Blackwater

I guess I'd been half expecting the shot; it slammed
through the kitchen window as I stood over the stove,
and thudded into the far wall. I turned and hit the floor,
waking myself as much as I could, and crawled to the
window and tried to reconstruct in my mind the way
things looked outside. The shot had come from across
the river, directed at the lighted window, so that made
tracking foolish and dangerous. I didn't think it meant
anything tonight—a warning but no more. The gunman
was probably riding half a mile into the brush by this
time. I said, "One for you, brave man," and went on
with my cooking. The shot did me a lot of good, to tell
the truth; it loosened me up . . .

I locked the back door, propped a chair under the knob,
scattered crumpled papers on the floor in the passage
between the store and the kitchen, and slept with both
guns under my pillow.

Books by Frank O'Rourke

Blackwater
The Professionals

Published by POCKET BOOKS

FRANK O'ROURKE

BLACKWATER

PUBLISHED BY POCKET BOOKS NEW YORK

POCKET BOOKS, a division of Simon & Schuster, Inc.
1230 Avenue of the Americas, New York, N.Y. 10020

Copyright 1950 by Frank O'Rourke
Copyright renewed © 1977 by Frank O'Rourke
Cover artwork copyright © 1987 Ken Laager

Published by arrangement with the author

ISBN: 0-671-63687-1

First Pocket Books printing June 1987

10 9 8 7 6 5 4 3 2 1

BLACKWATER

One

I HELD THREE TENS BEFORE THE DRAW AND THE STORE-keeper from the back country called my opening bet and raised me most of his stack. The other players dropped out and I called his raise. He drew two cards and I held a kicker for bait, hesitating long enough to give him the right feeling. Then I drew one. He studied his draw and checked to me. I bet him five hundred. He called and raised the balance of his stack, eight hundred more. I called the eight hundred and raised him two thousand. I wasn't worried. I'd drawn the case ten; it was my night.

His eyes were greedy and eager as he riffled his cards again and wondered how badly he had me whipped. He had a terrible poker face; or I should say just a terrible face. A one-eyed man with cataracts could see he had filled or made fours. But how big? He said, "Are we playing table stakes?"

"Bet anything you wish," I said. "Cows, chickens, horses, your barlow knife."

His face moved strangely through doubt and then a look of relief. He opened his wallet and showed us the deed and title to his store and quarter section of land in a little town named Blackwater. He said it was worth two thousand.

That was doubtful, but I told him, all right, I'd honor it as two thousand. He signed the deed and tossed it into the pot and laid down a big full house, three aces and a pair of queens. He reached hesitantly for the pot.

I said, "Sorry, friend," and showed him the forty-pipped beauty of four tens.

That was how I won the store. I knew better. I had disregarded the rigid laws of good poker, taking something I couldn't see or feel as legal tender. If that storekeeper had dropped out or had two thousand more in hard cash to meet my final raise, I would have taken his money and never seen the Spring Valley country; nor would I have experienced all that happened because of that store. I wondered that night at the strange look of almost blessed relief on his face when he said good night and left the room, a look entirely out of place on a man who had just lost his shirt. I understood him better a week later. But that was the chance. I broke the rules when I accepted his deed and I paid the penalty.

I was riding a long string of luck that night in Capitol City. I'd come up from St. Louis and before that from New Orleans; before that from all the towns where a man could shove his boots under a round table and draw cards in a big game. I had a racking cough in my chest; I was underweight; I drank too much between games; but my money belt was fat and my luck was riding for the wind.

Fate took a hand the next night.

We didn't have a storekeeper down from the brush for a whirl at the fancy life. We had a tough game. There were eight of us around the table in the Capitol Hotel that night: three other gamblers, two cattlemen named Ellender and Allen, and two wealthy townsmen. We had money to burn, food and drink whenever we signaled Mose, the colored porter; and I had my luck. I had never felt better. I had fifteen thousand dollars, not counting that store deed, and my luck seemed unbeatable—that is, until two in the morning.

We were playing five-card stud, the old army game. Eight men made stud a necessity. I dealt one of those hands a man has to play if he wants to keep his luck and, most important, his courage. If he backs down on such a hand, he's done forever. It went like this:

Three of us were playing before I dealt the last round. I had an ace down, an ace and two small cards up. Ellender had an ace and two small cards up. The case ace had not been dealt up around the table, but I knew Ellender had it in the hole.

He played with his cards and fidgeted with his cigar. He was a good poker player but he always dribbled ashes on the table when he held a big pair.

That's how it works.

We froze the others out with two big raises. I had to raise and Ellender had to call and raise back. We both had an equal chance to hit another pair or a high kicker card. When Ellender raised me the third time I pushed my stack in, the only way a man can play the game when his luck is good. Ellender called. I dealt. He got a king. I dealt myself a queen.

He had me whipped. That king was the kicker; it beat my queen. I knew it, he knew it, just as I realized my luck had run out and that store deed was the reason. Ellender said, "Are you all in, Stanton?"

"Sorry, Ellender," I said. "I'm all in."

And then I laughed. The humor of the situation, reversed from the past night, struck me. I said, "Unless you'd like to take a store deed from the back country. I accepted it for two thousand last night."

Ellender shook his head. "Sorry, Stanton. I think I've got you outkicked, anyway."

Ellender turned his hole card; it was the case ace. His

king was the topper. I got up, bowed around the table, and said, "Thank you for a pleasant evening, gentlemen," and refused their offers to loan me money, and went out and down the hall to my room.

That deed was an omen. I began coughing when I locked my door and took my first drink. I nearly lost my stomach and whatever lungs I still possessed. Perhaps that influenced me. I don't know, but it caused me to consider my health, my financial status, all the pieces of living suddenly important to a man when his luck has changed. I had a hundred-dollar bill in my valise. I had my diamond ring, my clothes and my guns. I could telegraph a dozen men and get money. The diamond was worth two thousand. I wasn't dead broke.

But that deed. I thought more about it, between coughing spells and spitting blood into six handkerchiefs.

The storekeeper had said his land was worth two thousand. It was property I'd never seen, in a country I didn't know. I needed fresh air and rest. Why not take the morning train to the end of the track and grab a wagon to this town of Blackwater, sell the store and land, buy a horse and outfit, and ride into the hills for a few weeks? I could ride north and west along the bend of the Big Muddy and make Deadwood in two months, riding in easy stages. Maybe I'd feel better then; and if I didn't, the chips were down and the hand was played. Who would mourn if they found a horse running wild in the badlands?

I said, "Heads we take a ride," and tossed my last silver dollar on the bed.

At seven that morning I was on the train for Weeping Water. That was end of track for the Northern and Western railroad, with nothing beyond but their surveyor parties and naked grade stakes, stretching thinly into the wild country that finally became Green Hills. The agent told me that

Blackwater was fifty miles beyond Weeping Water and the railroad hoped to reach or pass the town by the end of next summer's construction. Nothing much there, he said, looking at me and labeling me for what I was. I didn't bother to set him straight. He was right, except for the store.

I rode the combination freight-and-passenger train from seven that morning until eight the next morning, bumping and winding over a grade so fresh the grass had not returned to hide the raw earth scars made by the Irish workmen who had dug and sweated and died to lay this track. We stopped in a dozen small towns before we pulled away from the settled land and nosed into rolling hills that soon divided and became the shortening fingers of the long running ridges flowing north toward the Big Muddy. Two of the towns were meal-stops and I tried to eat and could down and hold nothing heavier than coffee. A woman with two small boys and a baby needed help during the night and got it unwillingly from me. She told me her entire story before I could change the diaper and excuse myself. She was from Maine, riding on this final stretch of train to join her husband in Weeping Water where he had bought a place and built what she called a "brown-front" to house them during the winter. She told me about a neighbor of theirs from Cape Ann who had put his family and household goods in a freight car and traveled all the way to Weeping Water the year before, keeping house in the car all the way and for two weeks after their arrival while the man found a place. People like this woman gave me a feeling of my own worthlessness, and I went to the smoker and stayed there the remainder of the ride.

I smoked my last decent cigar before we pulled into Weeping Water the next morning. Stepping down from that miserable train, I needed a smoke and a drink like the devil needs new recruits. On the last half-mile south of town I saw a boy on a pinto pony herding sheep on a sloping pasture, and the sheep broke at the engine whistle, running from the train with the boy kicking the pinto in the flanks and cracking it with a willow switch, hightailing after those blasted sheep and turning, his long yellow hair streaming behind him, to shout at the train and yell something I wished I could hear and never did. Maybe it was better not to hear a boy yelling from his pony; it made a man remember too far back and did him no good.

Weeping Water, even in late September, was a roistering madhouse of trade and building and general confusion. Settlers were pouring in from the East in their own wagons and on the train; and the railroad was easily the most prominent and permanent-looking part of the town. The shops and railroad turning triangle were south of the depot, with the work barracks lying grimy and squat beyond the shops on the river bank. The town proper, a hodge-podge of frame shacks, soddies and a few rawly new brick buildings, spread out north of the tracks and lurched clumsily up the lower slope of a long ridge. This town was a year old and showed its untried strength and rawness in the potholed, muddy streets, the rough-built store fronts, even the church with steeple and cross unfinished, looking gauntly above the houses on the north slope. I stood on the depot platform, getting my bearings, and saw trappers, cattlemen, farmers in for supplies, new settlers wandering aimlessly, storekeepers arguing with customers or with each other, women shopping, Indians down from the river reservations, all the heterogeneous assortment of human flesh you saw in a jump-off town. This place was fairly quiet now, with winter coming on, but next spring would bring back all the brawling and trouble that railroad work gangs and their camp followers could cause in a growing town at end of track. I could make money here during the winter and the spring. I knew that I counted ten saloons along their main street, and each of those would have its tables and wheels.

The woman with her two small boys and the baby passed me and smiled timidly. "It looks wild, don't it?"

I said, "Not bad, ma'am. Just natural."

She was looking eagerly across the street and then she saw her husband and I watched her face break and change into something any man would cherish and be selfish about even letting anyone else see. He met her a few feet from me, those little devils grabbing his pants and jumping, and they kissed each other, and he touched the baby and grinned. They started across the street toward a wagon with a high box top. She remembered me and turned and said, "Thank you again for helping me last night."

I lifted my hat and said, "The pleasure was mine, ma'am," and nodded to her husband.

He took one look at me, my clothes, and gave me a reluctant smile and led his family away. I wondered how long it would take him to explain some of the facts of this country to her, that she'd let a gambler change her baby's diapers and be so near her boys they might have been polluted. That was how it was, and nothing would change it. I watched them get into the wagon and roll toward the west, another part of this life I could see but never understand.

I saw a farmer talking with the implement dealer down the street on my side. They stood over a walking plow and the dealer was shaking his head and waving his arms, and the farmer kept turning away and looking wistfully at one of those new riding plows and I could almost repeat their words and thoughts. Walking plows were about fifteen dollars, I thought, and the riding plow would run around thirty-five, and that farmer was weighing values in his mind, comparing the ease of using the riding plow against the back-breaking work with the walker, kicking sticky, cling-

ing mud from the mold-board when the ground was wet,
sharpening the share every night, and yelling at his mule
and then being jerked and twisted when the mule took off
unexpectedly. Then he would think of the things he could
buy with the fifteen- to twenty-dollar difference—a few
panes of glass for his new house, maybe for his soddy,
nine by twelve at five cents each, or maybe something
larger if he cared at all for his wife's health, say twelve by
twenty-eight for twenty cents. Or he would be thinking of
a shotgun for eighteen dollars or an extra sack of beans or
rice at three cents a pound, or a couple of new tin pans
and a pot and a skillet for his wife. There were so many
things a man could wish for, want with all his heart, and I
thought how that farmer would make twenty dollars do the
work of a thousand the way I valued money. He bought
the solid things a man could feel. I bought the stuff no man
has ever felt with his hands. It was no good thinking this
way, but seeing the town and these people brought the old
memories again, fresh and never-fading. My curse was
simple; I knew too much and I could not forget.

I knew how this state was being settled. I had talked
with men in Capitol City, and they told me how the people
were pouring in from the East. Most of them were family
men. This was no gold rush. They brought their wives and
children in their wagons, or on the train, and they lived in
those wagons until they bought a place and built a rough
house. I knew the man in Capitol City who was making
a small fortune selling them ready-cut lumber to build a
house, if they had the ready money. They didn't need a
carpenter; all they needed was a hammer. They hauled the
ready-cut lumber to their place and put it up. The poor
ones built soddies. They plowed up this tough matted sod
and cut it into the thick bricks with a spade, and a good
man could throw up a fifteen-by-fifteen soddy in ten days.
They called them brown-fronts and they were warmer in

winter and cooler in summer than a wood house. God looks out for his poor, I thought. They could build a soddy from their own earth and if they were so poor they could not buy doors and windows in a town like Weeping Water, well, trees were theirs for the cutting along the rivers and creeks and circling the sloughs. Trees, even cottonwoods, make good rafters and studding when a man has to shift for himself. "Well," I thought on this morning, watching these people and this town, "this state will be a corker when it finds its legs and gets under way."

I went down the platform with these thoughts of the honest, decent people, my boots grinding on the black cinders and found the agent who told me to go around on Front Street and locate a freighter named Henry for my ride to Blackwater. The agent told me Blackwater had about three hundred people, was not yet a year old, and lay on the projected route of the railroad unless something happened during the winter and the big boys changed their minds. I didn't attach much importance to the agent's words that morning, but I remembered them well later. So I walked along Front and found the freighter named Henry checking harness on his three-team wagon, smoking a vile cigar and cursing his horses in a husky voice. He was a leathery man in his middle years, with bowed legs and heavy limbs and a face chewed and battered by time and made twice as piratical by a week's crop of dense black whiskers. He used one word in place of ten, and only grunted the rest of the time.

I said, "Blackwater?"

He said, "Five dollars."

I paid him and swung my valise on the wagon. He said, "I got another passenger."

"You've got room," I said.

He chewed that cigar and studied my clothes. He said, "Gambler?"

15

I was in no mood for trouble. I said sarcastically, "Now what makes you figure that?"

He said, "Clothes," and that was all the talking he did for a while.

We drove out Front. Henry cracked his whip and cursed his horses, urging them through potholes and around wagons, and pulled up suddenly before a big house on the edge of town. He shouted, "Miss Charlotte!" and a woman stepped out, said good-bye to an older woman in the doorway, and came down the boardwalk to the wagon, carrying a small valise and throwing a bright red scarf around her neck.

She smiled at Henry and said, "I thought you'd forgotten me," and Henry blushed under his whiskers and said gruffly, "I wouldn't forget you, Miss Charlotte," and then showed more speed than I thought he possessed, taking her valise and helping her to the seat.

I got off the seat and moved back on the load, balancing myself on boxes and sacks, and she gave me a pleasant glance and sat down. She was a small girl of twenty-two or -three, I judged, with a thin face and jet-black hair and a body that moved smoothly under her dress. She pulled the red scarf over her head and tied it under her chin, and Henry finally remembered me and jerked his head.

"This fella is ridin' along," he said. "Come on the morning train."

Henry didn't elaborate. I tried to bow standing up on a sack of onions and a box of shotgun shells. I lifted my hat and said, "Jim Stanton, ma'am."

She turned her head and murmured, "I'm Charlotte Bisonette, Mr. Stanton," and then she surprised me. She said, "We have plenty of room on the seat, Mr. Stanton. Won't you join us?"

Young ladies weren't supposed to sit with gamblers, let alone speak to them; when she spoke to me and smiled, I was too surprised to answer for a moment. She knew I was a gambler because she had two eyes; she could see my clothes, my face, my hands; and yet, she offered to share the seat. I wondered who she was and why she was so different. Henry was scowling and shaking his reins, and I made a quick decision.

"Thank you," I said, "but I've got a bad cough. I'd better ride here, Miss Bisonette."

Her eyes laughed at me and touched on my mouth and face, and then she said, "Very well, Mr. Stanton."

"Hup!" Henry shouted. "Hup, you devils!"

I crawled back on the load and wedged myself between sacks of onions and got as comfortable as I could, which turned impossible a mile from town, when we suddenly dropped off the passable road onto a winding, muddy trail filled with chuckholes and small rocks. Then I suffered. I was soft and that wagon seemed to conspire against my body, searching out and hitting every rock, dropping soddenly into every chuckhole, twisting and jarring me until I heartily cursed myself for being such a strait-laced fool and refusing her offer of the seat. I turned my back to them and held a handkerchief to my mouth, and tried to find the pitch and sway of the wagon so as to ride it out the best possible way.

We climbed a long ridge and came to the first table of a wide plateau, and Henry made fast time, whipping and cussing his horses, driving his wagon like a stagecoach. We had pulled out of Weeping Water at nine o'clock, and noon found us galloping along a narrow trail, up a valley flanked by rough hills, with the deeper blue of the Big Muddy bluffs silhouetted far to the north. A creek ran through the valley and the trail held to a steady upgrade on this stream's bank until we climbed abruptly to another creek and a ford. It was just noon and I estimated we had covered twenty miles.

I put my handkerchief away when we stopped on the gravel bar nosing down to the ford. Henry called, "Take a stretch. We blow 'em here."

I dropped heavily to the ground and stood beside the wagon, aching all over. I was dirty and I needed a shave and my lungs were two solid, heavy bags of pain in my chest. Charlotte Bisonette jumped down lightly and whipped off her red scarf and gave me a quick, wide-eyed smile. She reminded me, in those first moments of meeting, of an otter or a weasel. She was quick and light on her feet, and she had the swift, curving movement of such an animal. If I had been well, if other things were equal, in the city, on a boat, anywhere but here, she would have interested me long before this stage of the game. She was giving me encouragement, and I wasn't responding. But I was dirty and dog-tired and women were far from my thoughts.

She said, "Why, you're sick, Mr. Stanton. Are you sure it's just a cough?"

"No," I said. "I'm not sure."

"Oh," she murmured. "Don't you care?"

"A small matter, Miss Bisonette," I said shortly. "Time takes care of all our troubles."

"And sometimes magnifies," she said evenly. "How do you like our country?"

"Very nice," I said. I knew what she wanted. She was curious about me and my business, and she wanted to find out why I, a gambler, was going to Blackwater. I said, "A wild country, Miss Bisonette, but full of possibilities."

"I think so," she said quickly. "Are you planning a stay in Blackwater?"

"I don't know," I said. "I've never seen your town."

She nodded, a small flirt of her head that shook the black hair about her eyes and face in a shining mass. She ran to the creek and scooped a handful of water to her mouth.

Henry watered the horses with a professional touch and a sour stare in my direction, then jerked the leaders up short and said. "Time to shove on, Miss Charlotte."

That was all the conversation we had throughout the afternoon. We stopped ten miles beyond the creek at a halfway house, a soddy with a large stable behind; and Henry changed teams with the help of two dirty, indifferent hostlers who gave me dull stares and then turned to their work. Charlotte Bisonette stayed on the seat, watching them, and I hunkered down between my onion sacks and wished I was dead or in New Orleans, for each represented the extremes of a man's desire and I was in no mood for halfway measures. Changing teams took five minutes, and then we swung onto the trail and cut the dust.

The fresh horses jerked us along at a full gallop and Henry showed his inner character by whipping them up every rise and cursing them down the other side; and the hills grew taller and more conical, like sombreros marching against the sky, and I knew we were swinging in toward the Spring River again and not so far from the Big Muddy hills. At five o'clock we crossed the highest ridge of the ride and I looked down on the Spring Valley.

It was a view to take a man's breath, a sudden, unexpected change from the monotonous day's ride. The Spring River had made its wide swing west from Weeping Water, and turned north here to split the ridges and form a broad valley that extended, as I discovered later, all the way to the source of the river on the southern watershed of the hills that separated it from the Big Muddy. The valley was about five miles wide, I judged, with the eastern slopes higher than those to the west, where the land seemed to roll away into nothingness. We dropped into the valley and crossed to the west bank through a wide, very shallow ford, and then headed north toward the town. I noted that east of the river the land was dotted with farms, while to the

19

west was untouched land. I saw cattle grazing on those western slopes, well back from the river.

We were getting close. I called, "Let me off at Simpson's store, Henry."

Henry grunted, "Simpson's? Good thing you spoke up."

We were about two miles south of town and nearing the junction of a trail which crossed this main road from the west and followed a shallow cut to another, and apparently deeper, river ford, I saw a weather-beaten building on the river bank, facing the road conjunction; and Henry suddenly pulled in his horses in front of this building. I didn't understand.

Henry said, "Simpson's," and waited for me to get out.

I couldn't express myself decently right then. I tossed my valise to the ground and climbed over the left rear wheel. Charlotte Bisonette gave me a teasing, deliberately inviting smile and said, "I hope you enjoy your stay in Blackwater, Mr. Stanton."

"Thank you," I said. "I won't."

She didn't have time to answer that because Henry wasn't approving her conduct. He cracked his whip and I stood alone beside the dusty road, watching them careen toward town. I turned and looked at the store and thought, Two thousand dollars? Two thousand empty dreams! and went inside. The customer bell jangled somewhere in back, and a man came through the narrow connecting door from those quarters.

He was big and grossly fat, a bearded man with dirty hands and shifty, narrow eyes and uncut mousy brown hair that curled over his shirt collar in uneven drake tails. He said, "Yes, sir," and didn't seem to give a damn whether I bought anything, shot him in the stomach, or dropped dead at his feet. I didn't like his looks and I didn't like the store; and then I took a good look around and knew I'd been taken for a sucker.

"Cheese," I said, needing more time to think. "And crackers. You got any tomatoes?"

"Yessir," he said, moving behind the counter. "Just pull in, mister?"

"Just," I said. "Thirsty and hungry."

He said, "Old Henry drives awful fast," and pushed half a wheel of Longhorn cheese toward me and waved one dirty hand at the cracker barrel. I leaned against the counter, broke off some cheese and ate each piece between two dry, stale crackers; and downing this, cut off the tomato can lid with his counter knife and drank juice and rind, wiped my mouth and gave the store another look.

Two thousand dollars!

This building was about twenty-five by thirty in the store proper, with a few feet tacked on the rear for living quarters. The counter ran full length along the east wall, which was the river-bank side. On the west wall were a few odds and ends of bolt goods and work pants and cheap boots and cowhide work shoes. Behind the counter, on shelves so dusty I could see exactly where my tomato can had been a moment before, the empty spaces outnumbered the cans six to one. The stock was so low a man could load it in a wagon, take it down to the river, dump it, and watch everything disappear in thirty seconds. A dirty, dusty, unkempt store, as useless and stale and no good as its former owner who fooled me neatly and was probably high-tailing it for St. Louis right now.

I tossed the tomato can in the woodbox and said, "That's better. Now a drink and I'll feel like living."

"In town," he said. "Two saloons, the Big H and the Granger's Rest. Side by each."

"What do I owe you?" I asked.

"Which saloon are you drinkin' in today, mister?" he said.

His little eyes were jumping over my face and clothes and hands.

"Which one?" I asked. "The nearest to a man's mouth, the way I feel."

"Sure," he said. "Of course, you know which one that is?"

I hadn't liked his looks when I walked in; now I couldn't stand him. I said, "I'm a stranger. What difference does it make where a man drinks? It's a free country. My money has the color of all money. I'll take the nearest saloon if it worries you."

"The Granger's Rest," he said. "Are you thinking of farming then, mister?"

"And why?" I asked, wondering about this man, this town, and the way a stranger was questioned over the small matter of buying a drink even before he set foot in the town; and liking none of it before I got the drink and saw the town.

"The Granger's Rest is just that," he said. "For farmers. The Big H is cattlemen. Drink in one, you drink there the rest of your stay here, mister."

"And where do you drink?" I said.

He picked his teeth with a dirty fingernail and said, "The Big H, mister. Take my advice and try their liquor yourself."

I gave him all the rope in the world. I said again, "What do I owe you?"

He sighed and stroked both hands along the worn counter edge. He said, "Where are you drinking, mister?"

"Because you seem so worried about my health," I said, "I'll tell you. I drink where I please. You say the Granger's Rest is nearest. I'll take my first drink there. My feet are tired and my eyes hurt, mostly from seeing a lot of ugly things today."

His little eyes got bright and mean. I knew what he was

thinking. He was judging my size and saying to himself that here was a pasty-faced gambler, five-nine, one hundred and forty sick pounds, no fight in a man like that. He said, "No charge, mister. Just don't stop by again."

I said, "What's your name?"

"Higgens," he said. "If it makes a difference. Take your walk, mister. It's two miles to town."

I pulled the title from my pocket and held it under his nose. I said, "You know what this is?"

"Looks like a deed," he said.

I said, "Can you read?"

"Sure I can read."

"I doubt it," I said. "I'd better read it to you. Pack your duffel and get out of this dump and don't come back. Simpson lost this store to me in a poker game two nights ago. Until I sell, burn, or decide what to do with it, I'll manage by myself. Start moving, Higgens."

He could read. He saw that title and knew it was the true paper. He frowned and said, "Now wait a minute, mister."

"Get out," I said. "Before I throw you out."

That jarred him loose. He said, "You! Try it!"

He came around the counter so eager to grab me he knocked the cracker barrel over. Crackers flooded out and crunched under his boots. I let him come all the way out and then drew one gun from my right shoulder and centered it carelessly on his belt buckle and watched him skid and get so scared the yellow in his back faded all the way through to his face. He burbled and threw up his hands and said, "Wait—wait. I never meant no harm!"

"Pick up that barrel," I said quietly. "And the crackers. Then start packing. I'll just come along and watch."

Five minutes later I watched him run from the store and head for town at a dogtrot, his war bag banging against the small of his back with every step. I had the key. The store, such as it was, was all mine. Higgens wouldn't come back. But I wasn't finished with him. I knew that. I would be wise to shade the windows and stay inside during the nights I was here, and ride away in the night when I left this place. Higgens was a man who had courage when he could stake out and blow your head off with a rifle; and if you had courage it did you little good against a bullet from behind.

I didn't waste time looking over my property. I dropped my bag in the kitchen and went through the front door, locked it, and started for town. I was lucky then. I caught a ride with a farmer and so came into Blackwater for the first time on the bench seat of a wagon, sitting beside a farmer who wanted to ask me questions and was stumped because I wouldn't give him a lead. He was still waiting when I got off on the edge of town and called, "Thanks, friend," and took my own good time about entering. I stopped for a moment on the road, just south of the first house, and stared at the town and said, "Great God!"

This was Blackwater one year after the first nail had been driven into green lumber. A town of about three hundred people with one block of stores on the west side of Main, and the houses crowded in close around the stores, lonesome-looking buildings without paint in this stage of the town's brief life, as if these people were not sure of their own endurance or the town's future and were leery about spending a few extra dollars for the paint. The country around, the valley and then the hills, checkered the land in all directions, hemmed this town with their emptiness and gave it, even now, a wild and impermanent look. This town was so new the sidewalks were only twisted green board strips on each side of the dusty street, the stores thrown together haphazardly, the houses built not for permanence but for shelter. This was my first estimate of the town, and how wrong I was, and then again, how right in one respect, I learned quickly and bitterly.

I came into town and stopped in front of the first saloon, the Granger's Rest. I thought about Higgens and his warning. I needed that drink and then I coughed, spitting blood in the dust and all I wanted was one drink and two days of sleep.

I pushed through the swinging doors and found myself on the same creaky boards in the same dingy barroom. They didn't change much in the little towns on the edge of the wild country. Always the long room, smoky and never entirely cleared of spent dreams and cigar butts and sawdust in the corners where the swamper forgot to push his broom. A few tables and chairs, a bar with the brass rail, the back-bar mirror, a calendar or two, a few sales notices and whisky ads, and that big picture of the dubiously moraled lady reclining on purple robes. They were all alike. I stepped to the bar, noticing two other customers at the back table, and said, "Whisky, your best," and waited.

The bartender said, "Yes sir," and brought out his best and a glass. I poured a drink, took it neat, swallowed a cough, and paid him. I felt a little better. Then I turned and saw those two men watching me with a half-lidded, impersonal interest from that back table. One of them was long and hollow-chested, wearing work clothes and cowhide boots. The other one was skinny and short, with an underslung jaw and innocent eyes. His face betrayed his eyes; it wasn't innocent. They could be anything a man pinned on them, and probably were. I said, "Good liquor," and returned to the street.

I saw Charlotte Bisonette and a stocky, middle-aged man across the street in front of the general store; and then I saw the big man standing over the stocky one who was possibly her father. This big man was not talking about the weather, or making sheep eyes at the girl. He was talking to the little man in a loud, arrogant voice, and he had the physical equipment to back up his words. He stood at least six-two in his boots. He wore work pants, and a lumberjack shirt under a heavy leather jacket hanging open, with a flat-crowned black hat pulled low over his wide, fleshy face. He had a spatulate nose and a thick, wide mouth. The little man said something sharp and the big one swung one hand, open-palmed, in a gesture of rude strength, knocking the little man flat on his back into the dust of the street below the sidewalk. And then the big man laughed.

Charlotte Bisonette cried out, not words so much as anger, and turned blindly into the general store. I saw her through the windows, rushing for the gun rack, and I knew that she had the kind of courage you rarely find in a woman. I couldn't help myself. I knew better. I was moving into somebody else's quarrel, but this was something I couldn't dodge. I saw four big men far down the street in front of the lumber shed, and as I crossed over, these men started running toward us, their boots spurting gouts of dust behind them. I stood beside the stocky man, who was sitting up in the dust and wiping his face, and looked at the big one.

I said, "Why don't you use a club?"

He gave me the tag end of his laugh, his eyes green and unsmiling above that wide mouth. He said, "So?" and his mouth sobered and sneered at me. He wondered who I was and cared less than enough to ask.

"Move along," he said. "You made a mistake, stranger. We settle our troubles our own way here. Move along."

Maybe it was the way he spoke, or just the words, or his easy contempt for me, as if I didn't exist. I said, "Get a club. You can't do a good job without it, can you?"

"A club?" he said, and laughed shortly. "Me use a club. Why?"

Now he was watching me, looking for some more fun.

He was one of those big men who never had enough fun—when it was knocking little men on their backs and laughing at their helplessness.

"On me," I said. "Better get one for each hand."

"On you?" he said, and then he roared with laughter, throwing his head back, convulsed at this idea. It was funny to him, me barely five-nine and outweighed seventy-five pounds.

I said, "Try it, bucko," and waited for him.

I didn't have long to wait. He sobered quickly and moved toward me, big and fast for all his weight, those banana fingers curving happily for my neck. He was going to pick me up and shake me like a rat and spit in my face and throw me in the dust beside the stocky man. He'd show me what happened to strangers in his town; yes, by God, he was the big boy and he was rough and tough and ready. I let him jump from the sidewalk, his breath nearly in my face, and then I slapped him four times across that wide mouth, slammed my sharp boot toe against his shin, and dodged around him and up on the sidewalk.

I didn't have one chance in ten thousand to even sting him; but I made him cry with sudden, comical pain and grab his leg instinctively and dance up and down in the street, a ludicrous figure for a moment, a big man made foolish in the only way he could be shamed. Then he stopped dancing and got coldly furious; and when a man his size turned serious, the party was over. He said, "All right," with deadly meaning and came for me.

I drew both guns and held them low and waited. He was coming fast and he tried to stop, just like Higgens in the store. He was a pace from me, tied in a knot but unafraid, staring at my guns and wondering if I would shoot him in the stomach or break his kneecaps.

"Guns," he said. "I've got no gun on me."

"Get one," I said. "Get two. Put another under your

jaw. Stick a knife in your teeth and tie a rifle to each leg. I'll still be here.''

"So," he said, still unafraid.

He backed away and he wasn't looking for trouble now. He had business ten miles in the country. He'd just remembered that business and he was wishing he could speak a magic word and disappear in smoke and come down in the hills. But all he could do was back off, and then his boot heel stuck on the edge of the sidewalk and he lost balance and sat down in the street. I couldn't have played it better if I'd planned it for a month and made him rehearse six hours a day.

He got up, clothes dusty and twisted, and crossed the street to the Granger's Rest. The swinging doors rattled with the wind of his entry and then the street was quiet except for the now loud pounding of many boots as those four men rushed up and stood around the stocky man. Other people had come from stores and watched us, but they weren't having any part of this. Not them. They were just curious. The stocky man got up and brushed his clothes, and behind me, from the general store, Charlotte Bisonette rushed out with a double-barreled ten-gauge shotgun in her hands and stood beside him, saying, "Where is he, Dad! Where is he?"

He looked at me and nothing came from his mouth but a pleased and hoarse, "Ahhh!" as his eyes brightened and he became a man again, an expensively dressed small man with a feeling and look of power in his face. He touched her arm and pushed the shotgun muzzles toward the ground and murmured, "Thank you, girl. Take it back now," and then looked at me and said, "Friend, I'd like to thank you."

I said, "For what?"

"Doing something that needed doing for a long time!"

I said, "Is it done now?"

His eyes were still bright with anger, but thought and cold common sense controlled his mind. He said, "How would you answer that, you being a stranger?"

"This way," I said. "Go home, friend. Go home and cool off. You're not hurt. Neither am I. That's how far it goes with me."

One of his big men said, "Watch your tongue, stranger."

I laughed at him and my eyes looked at his gun and then at his eyes, and he got the point and shut up.

Charlotte Bisonette said, "May I thank you, Mr. Stanton?"

"You may," I said. "I suggest you take your father home and give him a tonic."

I thought she would burst out laughing right there, which was the last thing I wanted, even though I was deliberately angering all of them. But I had a thought, and I wanted to put something with that thought and reach an understanding of this town and these people; and the best way to get right in the middle of a fight is to make everybody mad at you. I lifted my hat and said, "A pleasure," and left them.

I caught a ride back to the store with that same farmer. I didn't open my mouth for two miles, and he swallowed his own thoughts until I got down and said, "Thanks, friend," and then he mumbled something and whipped his team to a gallop. He wanted no part of me. I wanted nothing more than sleep and rest, a meal, then sell this miserable store and ride away; and I found myself thinking of Charlotte Bisonette's face and mouth, and I knew the ride couldn't start too soon. I was so engrossed with these thoughts, and so tired, that I didn't see the girl at the door until I bumped into her. She spun around and then smiled at me.

She said, "Excuse me. Is Higgens here?"

She was taller than Charlotte Bisonette. She had a sweet, oval face and light-colored hair and her eyes were soft brown and gentle. She wasn't afraid of me. She wanted something in the store and she smiled as if getting gumped by strangers was all in the day's work.

I said, "My apologies, ma'am. Higgens isn't here. This is my store."

"Your store?" she asked mildly. "Where is Mr. Simpson?"

"I don't know," I said. "Did you want something, ma'am?"

"Pepper," she said. "Black pepper."

I grinned. "You know where it is, if there is any?"

I think she understood that I wasn't a storekeeper by profession. She smiled, showing even white teeth, and said, "I do, indeed," and when I opened the door and followed her inside and lit a lamp, she got a can of pepper from the lowest shelf behind the counter. She said, "I don't imagine you know the price, do you?"

"No, ma'am," I said. "Do you?"

"Ten cents," she said. She placed a dime on the counter.

I noted the bulging coin purse opened quickly and replaced in a pocket, and decided that here was a good cash customer. She looked at me again. "Mr. Simpson sold you the store?"

"Not exactly," I said. "I won it in a poker game."

"I see," she murmured. "Well, I must be going. Thank you . . ."

"Jim Stanton, ma'am," I said.

"I'm Mary Carr," she smiled. "I live half a mile up the road toward town."

That explained a girl like her coming to this store so late in the day. It was close and when she wanted something, she could get it half an hour faster than making a trip to town. I liked this girl immediately. She smiled without guile and she talked with a natural honesty that showed she didn't care if I were a gambler. I think my face showed my thought because she smiled again and said, "I wish you luck in your new business, Mr. Stanton," and went out.

I decided that was enough for this day; it was almost dark outside and I wanted to lock up and cook a meal and get some sleep. And come morning, I thought bitterly, I'd sell to the first fool I saw, for anything he'd offer, and get out of this town. I was halfway to the door when I heard horses coming at a run, then pulling up outside. The door opened and Bisonette came in. I saw his four men and Charlotte Bisonette outside, in their saddles, waiting for him. He wasn't lacking company now.

He said, "Mr. Stanton. A word with you."

"You're Bisonette," I said.

"Yes," he said curtly. "My daughter told me you rode up-river with her today."

I said, "Yes. . . ?" and waited.

Another horse galloped down from the north and turkey-trotted over toward the group outside. I heard someone call, "Hold up, Mixon," and the big man's voice, even and controlled now, answered, "No harm intended, Clancy. Just talk."

Clancy said, "If Miss Charlotte wasn't here . . ." and let his meaning lie between them, harsh and without alternative.

Charlotte Bisonette said sharply, "Don't mind me, Clancy."

Mixon said, "Evening, Charlotte."

She didn't answer him, and I heard him dismount and pass them and come to the door. Bisonette moved to the side and Mixon came in, saw him, looked at me, and closed the door. Bisonette said, "What do you want, Mixon?"

Mixon said, "I could ask you that, Bisonette. What do you want?"

Bisonette smiled and said, "Maybe the same thing. Let's ask Stanton."

I didn't like this. A lot of things I knew nothing about were running beneath the surface of their talk. I said, "Do your talking and get out."

"Ah," Bisonette said. "Where's Simpson?"

"Your business?" I asked.

"Yes," Bisonette murmured softly. "Mr. Stanton, is it true you now own this store and land?"

"It is," I said.

"You fired Higgens," Mixon said. "How come?"

"My business," I said. "Not yours."

"No," Bisonette said, just as soft, just as meaning. "Our business, Mr. Stanton."

"Stop the mush," Mixon said. "Stanton, what we mean is, who are you selling your goods to?"

Bisonette said, "You took a drink in the Granger's Rest."

"And then pulled down on me," Mixon said. "How come, Stanton?"

They were trying to say something and I couldn't untie the knot of words and find their meaning. It concerned this store, I knew that, but how, and in what way the store and I fitted their talk, I could not understand.

I said, "I don't follow you. I won this store in a poker game, if you want to know how. I came out here to sell it. I'll sell to the highest bidder. I don't care who buys it. I'm tired. I want to sleep and then I want to sell this store and get out of this stinking town. Does that answer your questions? If not, get out anyway. If you can't understand plain talk, go wash your ears and come back in the morning. Maybe you'll understand then."

"You talk big," Bisonette said softly. "One man."

"Call them in," I said, "Go on, call them in. Five minutes from now, if you still think foolish talk is going to bluff me, if you're still hanging around, I'll reserve the first slug for you, Bisonette.''

Bisonette wasn't used to people slamming into him like this; I could see the anger churn in his face. Then he got control of himself. He said, ''I'll give you whatever you paid for it, Stanton.''

''That was two thousand,'' I said.

Mixon said, ''I'll make that three.''

''Four,'' Bisonette said, without hesitation.

They glared at each other. I watched them and said to myself, ''Four?'' and then I started thinking. I said, ''You heard me. Get out. Come back in the morning and talk business.''

They opened their mouths and I said, ''You hear me the first time?'' and put my fingers on my coat lapels. Mixon said, ''All right, bantam,'' and went outside. Bisonette paused long enough to murmur, ''I'll top any offer he makes,'' and then he was gone. I heard Mixon say, ''Just keep your hands off my horse, Clancy,'' and then the night was filled with galloping hoofs. Mixon rode toward town and Bisonette and his daughter and men angled west on the road that disappeared into the hills. Hoofs were loud, then died in the night.

I said, ''Now what the . . . ?'' and locked the front door and went through the store to the back rooms.

Simpson had built a kitchen and bedroom on the back end of the store. The kitchen was big and held a stove and table and cupboards and five chairs. The floor was bare wood with cracks showing the ground beneath. The bedroom was smaller than the kitchen, just large enough for a bed, a few wall hooks, a single window with an inside shutter which I closed and latched, and one chair beside the bed. I pulled the blankets back, raised the mattress and inspected for livestock. The bed was clean. Then I went into the kitchen, found ham and eggs and a loaf of home-made bread somebody had given Higgens; and using this for a base, and raiding the store for potatoes, peas, and dried apricots, I cooked a passable supper.

I guess I'd been half expecting the shot; it slammed through the kitchen window as I stood over the stove, and thudded into the far wall. I turned and hit the floor, waking myself as much as I could, and crawled to the window and tried to reconstruct in my mind the way things looked outside. The shot had come from across the river, directed at the lighted window, so that made tracking foolish and dangerous. I didn't think it meant anything tonight—a warning but no more. It was Higgens, no doubt of that, and he was probably riding half a mile into the brush by this time. I said, "One for you, brave man," and went on with my cooking. The shot did me a lot of good, to tell the truth; it loosened me up.

While I ate, keeping out of window line, I took another look at the title. I read once more that it included a quarter section of land with the store, one hundred and sixty acres which Simpson had bought, clear title, from a homesteader named Klug three years ago, for two dollars an acre. That meant nothing to me now; I would have to get outside and find the boundaries to make sense. Even that wouldn't help a great deal. Fence lines mean nothing much when the price was already beyond logical understanding. I locked the back door, propped a chair under the knob, scattered crumpled papers on the floor in the passage between the store and the kitchen, and slept with both guns under my pillow.

---------------------------- Two ----------------------------

I HEARD THE THUNDEROUS KNOCK BEFORE I WAS FULLY awake the next morning. My chest was thick with pain and my lungs were a dry fire that gave my mouth a parched taste. When the knock vibrated the entire building, I grunted painfully and tried to burrow away from the sound. Whoever it was changed tactics and came to the kitchen door and hit it a blow that rattled my bed. Failing there, he walked to my bedroom window and drummed a tune on the glass and finally slammed both open hands against the wall. I sat up, holding both guns on the open window and pulling myself against the wall, out of fire line.

I said, "Who is it?" and the words hurt my chest.

"Dan Hannigan," a voice roared. "Open up!"

"Hannigan?" I said. "Never heard of you. What do you want?"

"You running this store?" Hannigan shouted.

"Not now," I called. "I'm closed."

Hannigan's answer to this was another timber-cracking smash against my outer wall. Then he called, "It's noon and I need supplies and I don't figure on going to town for 'em. You get up or I'm coming through your front door and help myself."

He didn't sound mean. He was more like a big healthy farmer growling at me with sheer good humor and deviltry busting inside him; and he was undoubtedly the kind who would knock my front door down and help himself, just to show me he wasn't a man to joke about a promise. I grinned for no reason, and raised my voice:

"Listen, Hannigan," I called. "You hunker down on my front step and I'll let you in when I'm good and ready. Now start chasing your nose before I put twelve holes through that wall and write my name on your belly."

He shouted something that came out, "Ho!" and I heard him running toward the front door. I got up and spent five minutes dressing and washing and putting on a pot of fresh coffee. I started to take a drink and thought, why? and shoved the flask back in my valise. Then I kicked the crumpled paper aside and went through the store to the front door, pulled it open, and said, "All right, Hannigan. Come in or stay out."

The biggest man I ever saw in my life, barring a circus freak, ducked through the door into my store. He was five inches taller than Mixon and so wide his shoulders rubbed both sides of the door frame. His arms were long and heavy, and the hands dangling on the wrists were wide and meaty looking, but somehow managed to look graceful. His legs were tree trunks and his feet were three times my size. On an average man those feet would have been cause for laughter. The only other pair I'd ever seen like them were clumsy and grew on a big stevedore in New Orleans. On this Hannigan the feet looked natural.

That was his body. His head was big and well-shaped, resting on a size twenty neck if it was an inch, and he grinned down at me with all the laughter in the world reflected in his mouth and eyes. His nose was broken and had a hook in the middle that ducked off to one side, and his mouth was wide and full and, when I knew him better, forever trembling with silent laughter. He had fine teeth, big and not as white as they were yellow, but straight and solid. On this morning he was wearing a pair of old brown pants that barely reached the tops of his huge cowhide boots, a darned and faded blue shirt, and a black hat with a hole in the crown and a turkey feather stuck jauntily in the sweat band. This was Dan Hannigan the morning we met, the bravest and strongest man I ever knew.

He took three steps that carried him past me to the counter, where he broke off half a pound of cheese, ducked his other hand into the cracker barrel, mixed up cheese and crackers willy-nilly, and shoved most of it in his mouth. He turned then, chewing with those big yellow teeth, and grinned at me carelessly. He looked careless; that was as deep as it went. His light-blue eyes were too sharp. He was one of those men who never missed a stick, a stone, an upturned leaf. He wasn't a businessman, a city dweller, and he wasn't formally schooled in the fine art of gentle living, but here, in the open land, he was his own master. It was a good thing he passed me when he came inside; if he had stopped and looked down when he came through the door, I'd have been too flabbergasted to speak. Now I had time to recover my breath and my sense of proportion, and appreciate him for what he was.

"I'll be. . ." I said. "Where'd they find you, Hannigan? On top a mountain?"

"Secret," Hannigan said. "Anybody found there, they'd go back and get some more like me. Then I couldn't lick everybody in the world. What you holding that gun for, Stanton?"

His grin disarmed me, I was still holding my right gun, forgotten now as I watched him. I shook my head helplessly and holstered it. I said, "What's on your mind, Hannigan?"

"Nothing much," he said. "Just a look at you, Stanton."

"You got me up for that?" I asked.

"Nope," he laughed. "Not entirely. I wanted to see what kind of a man could clean Simpson at poker and then brace Mixon and Bisonette all in the same wiggle."

"You've had your look," I said. "Pass your judgment."

"Slow down," Hannigan grinned. "That'll take some time. Like you settling that trouble you had last night."

"News travels fast here," I said dryly. "Considering their primitive means of communication."

"Mary told me," Hannigan said simply.

"Mary. . . ?" I said. Then I remembered. "Miss Carr? A friend of yours?"

"My girl," Hannigan said. "I was going home from her place last night when Mixon and the Bisonette crew took out. Were they bluffing you down?"

"What do you think?" I asked.

"I think no," Hannigan said. "Do I smell coffee?"

"Can you cook?" I asked.

"Passable," he grinned. "I cook my own meals and I'm still kicking."

"Got work to do?" I asked.

"Me?" Hannigan said, in a hurt voice. "This late in the day?"

"All right," I laughed. "Come on back, Hannigan. You can cook breakfast."

We didn't get to breakfast for some time. Hannigan heard the horses before I did, and bent his head, listening to the drumming beat of hoofs coming from the west. He said, "You got company," and leaned against the counter and looked pleased. He was expecting something, but whatever it was he kept any explanation to himself. He chewed cheese and crackers, and the horses thundered down the long hill from the west and clattered into the front yard and milled around the hitching rail.

I recognized Bisonette's hat and shoulders through the window, and saw the four men he'd had with him the night before, only today he had brought along three more. That made seven of them and Bisonette, all paying me a visit. I looked at Hannigan and said, "You drawing cards in this deal?"

"I'm eating cheese and crackers," Hannigan said. "I'm a customer in your store."

I said, "Just stay that way, Hannigan, and don't forget to weigh that cheese."

The door opened and Bisonette came into the store, blinking his eyes against the inner shadow. He saw me first, smiled briefly and said, "Good morning, Stanton." His glance moved around the store and lighted on Hannigan. He said, "Hannigan!" and I knew how things stood between them.

Hannigan said, "Howdy," and kept on chewing.

Bisonette's men trooped inside and ranged themselves behind him, interested in shelves and their boot toes and each other, rolling cigarettes and wiping their faces with their bandannas and acting like everyday customers. One of them, the big man called Clancy, saw Hannigan and frowned.

I said, "Good morning, Bisonette."

"I'd like a few words with you, Stanton," Bisonette said. "In private, if you don't mind."

He wasn't worried about me, that was plain to see. I was a gambler on the trail, just another sharper going through from nowhere, stopping off for a quick deal and melting again into nowhere, wherever that beyond happened to be. He wanted to have a few words with me, make me an offer I couldn't refuse, and bid me goodbye. I didn't like his words and I didn't like his attitude.

"This is all right," I said. "What's on your mind?"

He frowned. "I said in private."

"This is private," I said. "Start talking."

Hannigan chuckled, a low sound in the stillness. Bisonette gave him a hard look and moved one shoulder. Clancy took a step toward the counter and leaned against its front corner, fingers on his belt, watching Hannigan.

"Hannigan," Bisonette said evenly. "Would you mind stepping outside for a few minutes?"

Hannigan held two crackers and a piece of cheese between his forefingers, balancing them delicately and forming a sandwich. Hannigan said, "I would," and pushed the sandwich between his teeth and bit down. The sound was a harsh crunch. Hannigan smiled cheerfully and didn't move.

I said, "If it's the same business, Bisonette, that's no secret. Get on with it."

Bisonette wanted to do something about Hannigan. I guess he made a mental count of his men and decided seven wasn't half enough to handle Hannigan. I silently agreed with him. He said, "Has Mixon been out yet?"

"Not yet," I said. "So squat down and relax, Bisonette. We'll wait till he comes."

Bisonette didn't like that at all. He said, "Never mind Mixon. I'll make you an offer he can't match, let alone top."

Somebody had to upset the applecart sooner or later, and this was my store and my deal, and I had a right to know what was going on. "Why?" I asked.

That one word seemed to lay a chill over the room. Bisonette's face surged with anger. Clancy's fingers played a little tune on his gun belt. Hannigan stopped chewing and waited expectantly for more speech. Whatever the answer to my question was, it was important to every man in the room.

"Stanton," Bisonette said, "I don't think that makes any difference to you. You won this store in a poker game. You have no interest in this country. Why don't you sell for a good profit and ride on?"

Nobody had answered my question. It made me stubborn. I said, "What's a good offer?"

"Four," Bisonette said. "That's what I told you last night."

I shook my head. Bisonette said, "Be reasonable, Stanton. I'll make it five and no more. Take that or else."

I said, "Or else?"

The horses nickered and hoofs drummed a flat rataplan on the dusty main road. Bisonette was silent. They all turned and looked outside. I saw Mixon and two men ride up, dismount and flip their reins over the rail, and come toward the door. I recognized the two men. They were the loafers I'd seen in the Granger's Rest the day before, the short one and the tall one. They flanked Mixon, walking in a line, hands close to their guns, and entered the store in this way, Mixon first and both of them fanning out beside him.

Mixon put a shoulder against one of Bisonette's men and twitched a little, and that man staggered off a good three feet. Mixon looked around the room and saw Bisonette and me and, finally, Hannigan. Mixon looked rested this morning, as if he'd had twelve hours' sleep without a worry in the world.

He said, "Morning, Stanton. The bidding started?"

"Just," I said. "You want a hand?"

"Deal me in," Mixon said easily. "What's your open, Bisonette?"

Now I could feel, more than yesterday, the antagonism running hot between these men. There was something big in this miserable store of mine, so big it had scared Simpson clean out of the country, so big it touched Hannigan,

41

and so important it brought the two big men of this country to me, not me to them.

I said, "Four's the bid, Mixon."

Mixon said, "Five."

Bisonette had a wealth of temper running in him; it leaped in the thin pinch of his mouth and the wide-set black eyes and the way his shoulders came up and made a stiff and even line below his neck. He was a little man with a giant's temper and a big whip to back it up. He didn't like any part of this business. I wondered fleetingly if they would start shooting, and then I knew they wouldn't. It hadn't gone that far. I'd stepped in before the shooting stage was set.

"Six," Bisonette snapped.

Mixon smiled. "Seven."

"Eight!" Bisonette came back.

Mixon wasn't smiling so broadly. He said, "Nine."

"Ten," Bisonette said. "Keep going, Mixon. I'm not out of my penny purse yet."

Hannigan broke the tension. From the counter, well back from all of them, he said softly, "What you bidding, boys? Mules or tobacco plugs?"

I couldn't help myself. I laughed loudly.

Bisonette said, "What's so damned funny, Stanton?"

"You," I said. "And Mixon."

"Funny," Mixon murmured, no smile on his face now. "There's nothing funny about money, Stanton. Not big money."

"Not money," I said. "Both of you. You've got the brains of an owl between you. What kind of fool do you think I am? You come out here and start throwing money at me, you outbid each other. And why? For this rotten store building and stock worth nothing? For something worth a few hundred? You give away your hands to me before we draw cards. Do you think I'd sell this place now, before I take a good look around? If it's worth ten thousand to you, and God only knows how much higher you'd go before we started ducking lead, it's worth more to me to keep it a while. I'll just do that. I'll keep this store until I find out what the game is. So stop the bids. The sale is closed. Sorry I caused you a dry ride. I'll let you know when I want to talk business again.''

Hannigan said, "Well, well!"

I didn't know whether I was glad about Hannigan being behind me or not. He didn't have a gun, but then, I wasn't sure how he stood. Mixon took a quick look on each side of him, and his two men tightened their shoulders. Bisonette stared at me, unbelieving. He couldn't swallow so much, so fast. He was the big man in this country and he'd made a fine gesture riding all the way from his ranch to give a sick gambler good money for worthless property. Now the gambler was keeping the property, and his money was worth less than dirt. He was enjoying only one satisfaction now; Mixon was in the same saddle. I watched both of them, gave them a few moments to absorb everything, and then said, "I'm closing up, men. Sorry."

Mixon moved first, stepping away from the door and looking past me at Hannigan. He said, "Hannigan, have you been telling Stanton a bunch of lies?"

Hannigan moved from the counter behind me. I could tell that; the floor seemed to shift and dance a happy jig. Hannigan said softly, "Go home, Mixon."

Bisonette was thinking and his men were waiting, watching him. He said, "Stanton, you want a hand in this game, all right, you'll get a hand. You've got a week to get out of this country. One week! You hear me?"

"Friend," I said. "You've got one minute to get out of this store."

"And me?" Mixon asked.

"The same for you," I said.

43

I watched Bisonette's right hand. He held it close to his side and as Mixon spoke, he turned the fingers out in a fanning motion. I drew both guns and stepped back until my boots tapped the edge of the stove platform. Clancy had started his draw and I held one gun on his belt buckle. He pulled his hand from his gun and stood stiff, his face coloring with surprised anger. Bisonette looked at me and turned to Clancy, then to his other men, and said. "Well . . ." and stamped his boot on the floor. Mixon hadn't moved. Neither had his two men. Mixon wasn't scared. I knew that from the day before. He was the man I'd want to watch every moment. Wherever he came from, whatever he'd been in the past, he'd handled plenty of guns and knew how to respect them.

I said, "Keep thinking, Bisonette. I know what you're thinking. You can take me. But you don't like the odds. Turn your boys loose, Bisonette. I'll give you a gilt-edge guarantee you get the first three right in the stomach. The next two for Mixon, the other scattered around."

That was the only way to talk to those men. Stop them cold in the beginning and then put a thought in their heads and let them juggle it for a moment. And while they were standing motionless, wanting no part of my guns, Hannigan moved behind me. I didn't hear him until he was beside me.

"You said one minute, didn't you?" he asked.

"One," I said. "Time's up!"

"Just keep an eye on 'em," Hannigan murmured pleasantly.

I couldn't stop him. He crossed behind me and grabbed the man on the far side. He threw that man completely across the front of the store with one easy swing of those great arms. That man knocked two more down, and all three of them fell in a tangled pile of arms and legs, behind

Mixon and against the closed door. Hannigan said, "Now boys!" and there was no mistaking that tone.

"Clancy," I said. "Hold it!"

Clancy was one of those men who believed in his own skill with a gun because he'd had some success locally. Clancy was fairly fast, but only locally. I stopped his draw and held him with one gun, and then Hannigan took over the party. Nobody thought about drawing a gun after Hannigan reached that first man on the east side of the store. I saw a stampede for my door equaled by nothing on the trail to Abilene; and as the door would allow only one man to leave at a time, Hannigan had a field day. Mixon got out first. I saw him pull the door open, gauge Hannigan's rush, and then run outside and head for his horse. Mixon was a big man, and plenty tough, but just then he wanted no part of Hannigan.

Hannigan lifted one arm and dropped a clenched fist on a man's head, and the man went down and stayed on his face, never moving. Hannigan reached Bisonette, who had not moved, and picked the little man up with the other arm and held him full length, a foot from the floor, and laughed in his face. Hannigan said, "You're safe, little man," and dropped Bisonette and went after the others.

He caught five of them inside the door. It was like a boy smashing pumpkins with a plum club. Hannigan swung those big arms carelessly and men bounced and flew from him, ricocheting off the walls and the door, rolling on the floor. Hannigan forgot about the door being too small for him. He surged outside and took the casing with him, and with the splintered boards falling from his shoulders, overtook three of them as they ran for their horses. He slammed two of them together, heads knocking, and dropped them as he ran for the last one in the yard. He pulled that one from his horse, gave the saddle a yank, and threw the horse to its knees. Then he lifted that one above his head and threw him into the water trough. Then he dusted his hands and walked toward the store. Mixon was a quarter mile down the road, riding at full run, not looking back.

I said, "Bisonette, get your men and get out of here. I can talk to Hannigan but I can't control him."

Bisonette couldn't speak. Hannigan had done him a worse wrong than shooting him, or half-killing him with the fists. Hannigan had called him a little man. Bisonette walked past me, made a wide circle around the approaching Hannigan, got on his horse, and rode west. Hannigan came inside and looked around and grinned. I said, "Thanks."

"A pleasure," Hannigan said. "Here, I'll just toss these boys outside."

He collected the sleeping beauties by their collars and dragged them through my ruined door, and deposited them in a neat row beside the water trough. One of them woke up and saw him and screamed, and Hannigan said, "Get going!" and came back to the store.

"All right," I said. "You can start work any time you feel like it."

"Work?" Hannigan said. "What kind of work?"

"My door," I said. "And about two dollars' worth of cheese and crackers. You want to pay cash or work it out?"

Hannigan looked at me boyishly, and then we both laughed. He pushed his right hand out and we shook firmly. Hannigan said. "You're a gambler."

"Was," I said. "Still am."

"Crooked or straight?" he asked.

"Straight so far," I said. "Why?"

"So far?" he said. "The way you look, not much longer. You'll be dead. You're a sick man."

"Maybe," I said. "Let's talk about this store."

He said, "You don't know nothing about this country, do you?"

"Nothing." I admitted. "But I can learn."

46

"Why?" he asked.

"You tell me," I said. "You didn't come over today to eat cheese and crackers."

Hannigan grinned. "You took your first drink in the Granger's Rest. Then you stuck your nose into somebody else's business and made Mixon back water. Then you kicked both of them out last night. You finished things today. You sure started on the wrong foot around here."

"I did?" I said. "Now how do you figure that?"

"Mixon is president of the Grangers in this valley. Bisonette is the big rancher. Does that tell you anything?"

We were both playing with questions and answers, but both of us were too busy asking questions to bother with answers. Hannigan wanted to trust me and he was holding a lot of answers under his tongue; he wasn't sure of me yet. His thoughts were plain on his big, rough face. He wasn't a man skilled at hiding his emotions. He'd make a terrible poker player. But I liked him. He judged a man by what he saw, and he had a powerful and simple perception that even his apparently inept questions couldn't mask. He wanted to tell me a lot more and he wasn't sure; and he was wishing he could tell me, and get my answer.

"Not a thing," I said. "What they are makes no difference to me."

He said, "You going to sell this land and the store?"

"That's my business," I said.

"I know it," he said. "I was just trying to trick you." He grinned sheepishly. "I'm not so good at that, am I?"

"No," I said. "And while we're talking in circles, tell me about a man named Higgens. How would he settle a grudge?"

"He's a coward," Hannigan said. "He might pot-shoot you from a thicket but he'd run like a rabbit in the open."

"All right," I said. "This leaves us exactly where we

started. Except for one thing. Thanks for backing me today.''

"Ah," he said. "That was fun."

He hesitated a moment, thinking about something else and finally making a decision. He said, "Don't sell, Stanton."

"Is that an order?" I asked.

He looked foolish. "You know I can't order you, Stanton."

"You're big enough," I said.

He looked at my coat. "No bigger when you wear them."

"The others had them," I said. "That didn't worry you."

"You're different," he said softly.

We were still talking in circles. I said, "Get to the point."

"Sure," he said. "I'd like to come over tonight and talk."

He wanted to go home and think about me all day, and then make his decision and come back and either tell me all the things I didn't know, or maybe tie me in a square knot and throw me fifty miles east across the river. I said, "Fine. But sing out loud and long so I won't get nervous and shoot the door into your mouth."

"All right," he said. "Say, you want me to fix up that front door?"

"If you don't," I said, "you won't be visiting me tonight, Hannigan."

He stared at me and then said, "I think you mean that, Stanton," and went to work. He found a hammer and saw and nails, and repaired the front door while I cleaned up the store; and all the time he sneaked glances at me. He finished about three o'clock and I knew he was burning with some question he wanted to ask and was afraid to put at me.

I said, "Ask it."

He got red and tossed the tools inside the door and said, "You're reading my mind. I was wondering about those guns of yours."

"What about them?" I asked.

"I never saw any like 'em before," he said. "I'd like to know more about 'em."

Then I knew he never missed a thing. He hadn't seen them close up, only in my hands while he was plenty busy himself. I said, "How do you know they're different?"

"I can tell," he grinned. "That's all."

I wondered if he had some purpose behind this innocent talk. If he had, the best way to trip him was to string along. I said, "All right, here they are."

I drew them and held them out in my hands. He looked at me in surprise and finally lifted them and his big fingers closed around the butts and engulfed them. He said, "What . . . no, not .44s. What are they? They're balanced like a feather on a razor's edge."

"It's a long story," I said. "If you want to hear it, I'll make it short as I can. Stop me if you get tired listening."

His eyes gave him away. He'd listen to gun talk all night and the next day, and never get bored. He would be like that, I thought, so big a man he couldn't place much stock in guns, so big he hadn't bothered to learn about them, hand guns I mean. If Hannigan was good with guns, it was rifles.

"They're special guns," I said. "I won them from a man in St. Louis. He had them made in Pennsylvania by an old gunsmith named Brenner. His name is on the plates—there on the barrel, the left side. They're .36 caliber built into .44 frames. They've got a shorter barrel by half an inch than the regular .36 Navy Colt made by that

Colt London factory. The man told me he had one of those guns and gave it to this old man, and the old man told him to come back in six months, and when he went back there they were. I didn't think much of them for a couple of weeks after I won them—that was six years ago—but I discovered they're the finest guns I've ever shot.''

"But a little old bullet like that," he said. "That won't do no damage to a man. If you're bound to have a .44 frame whyn't you have the .44 bullet too? That'll knock anybody kicking.''

"Wait," I said patiently. "I've got my own ideas on guns, especially on that subject. Some of them sound like they contradict each other, but they all work out. Now you take a lot of men with guns. They think you have to have a .44 or bigger to get results. Then they think the hip draw is the only draw. They think the best way to kill a man is draw their blunderbuss and bang away. That's not true. But neither is it all false. Now take a .36 like this in its original form. The caliber is big enough to kill a man if you can shoot straight. All right, that's fine. We'll assume that. But to me, it's too light. I'm a small man but I can handle a .44 frame just as easy as a .36 and it feels better in my hands. Now, here's the first catch.''

"You mean the .44 kicks," he said. "I sure know that. I can't even hold one down.''

"That's it," I said. "The .44 is bound to kick, no matter how strong your hands are, no matter how many tricks you know about your own gun. But take this .44 frame and put a .36 action and slug in it and what have you got? You've got weight for steadiness, with less recoil than the .44. I found that out when I started shooting these guns. I can draw and fire just as fast with the .44 frame, and once I'm on the target and shooting, and I mean shooting, I'm steady on and holding true. The .44 frame gives me the weight for steady shooting, and the .36 slug gives me very little kick. I'll always thank that man for being a fool with two pair."

"Listen," he said. "Do you aim when you shoot? I mean, drawing from the shoulder like you do?"

"That's another argument they'll never settle," I said. "The best way to put it to you is tell you something I heard after the war. I was in a gunshop in Virginia City and I heard this clerk giving a young fellow some advice about guns. He told the young fellow about the four main points of shooting, as he called them. The draw, the aim, the fire, and the recoil. That was fine. Well, he was selling the young fellow one of those .36s, and he told him some of the things I've told you, about too much recoil on a .44 and how the .36, if you shot it true, would kill just as dead. This clerk said that he'd heard a lot about hip and fan shooting and how somebody must have shot that way, but mostly there were only monuments commemorating the results. That anything a man hit that way was pure accident, that the only and best way to shoot was from the shoulder draw and bringing the sights in line with the target and your eye, to do it quick as you can but not too fast. Now that was pretty good advice, with a few differences, as I see them. First, that clerk hadn't seen many hip shooters when he said they couldn't shoot, and shoot .44s. I've seen a few of them, and they were good. I said good, and I mean just that. Maybe they couldn't get the best results with second shots, or more, but their first one was in there to kill, and their second and third and more shots were too close for old age. There are plenty of monuments commemorating the results of their shooting, and a lot over the ones who shot like the clerk said, but a few of the shooters are still alive and the monuments they put the bodies under are scattered from Montana to Texas and from St. Louis to Frisco. On the whole, the clerk was right in a left-handed

way. But let's go on to what he told the young fellow about
bringing the sights into line with the target and your eye.

"The way that will probably be told in stories a long
time from now is how the young fellow went and practiced,
and got so good he could hit a playing card in no time at
all, according to the writer, and pretty soon he was so good
he could hold down a town marshal or gambling hall watch.
That's fine in stories, but not in truth. What I mean is, it
was possible for the young fellow to shoot like that if he
practiced, but not in the time the writers like to have you
think they learn. It doesn't take you weeks or months. It
takes years, and you never learn everything, you never get
as fast as you want, and to get to the point, you'll never
get fast enough if you line up the sights with the target and
your eye."

"I don't get that," he said. "How do you mean?"

"This," I said. "You can draw and shoot fast that way
but not as fast as really shooting with your whole body.
That clerk maybe didn't consider something like sitting at
a table and drawing on a man across the table or across the
room. It takes time to draw from the shoulder and line up
with your eye along your sights on the target and then
shoot. Maybe if you were good enough and had practiced
a long time, a terribly long time, then you could draw and
shoot from where you drew without raising the gun that
extra foot or so to eye level. Maybe it would mean the
fraction of a second that young fellow could never save if
he shot the clerk's way, if he didn't take the time and
patience to learn to shoot with his whole body."

"Sure," Hannigan said tightly. "I see. But it takes a
long time, don't it? Can you do it that way?"

I said, "I do it that way. I'm still here."

"Sure," he said slowly. "Sure, you're still here. But
how long did it take you?"

"Fifteen years," I said. "Right to now. And I still want

to be better. I learned shoulder shooting from my father first. After he . . . Later on I learned some more from a lot of men. It took me ten years to draw and shoot the way I wanted to, I mean, lying down or on either side, in a room or outside or downhill, or uphill, crosswind, any way. I guess you call it feeling your shots. You start shooting and you think you'll never get it, you work on your guns until they fit you, everything fits, the butts, the trigger pull, balance, learning the recoil, the proper powder loads, a thousand things. Then one day you finally get that feeling. Your whole body works together aiming your gun and you don't have to sight on eyeline to do it. You save that time. It might mean your life. Mostly, it does. What it is all together is, your hand and wrist and forearm get together with your eyes and your whole body, and they aim the gun on the target. You could call it a problem in geometry, but don't worry about it. Your own body is a better professor in this case than all the theorems in the world. A professor of mathematics would show you why it works by quoting a lot of stuff about triangles and things called parallelograms and perspective and angles and other things, but it all boils down to the fact that your eyes and body work the problem faster than you could even figure it out on paper, and after you practice long enough your eyes and body do it automatically. That's all. There's no easy way to do it. It's plain hard work. And it's not worth the work in the grief it'll give you in return.''

He handed me the guns and shook his head slowly, and said, ''I reckon you know your guns. Would you. . . ?''

''Come on,'' I said. ''You don't have to beg me. I'll show you anything you want. Let's go outside.''

He started to grin then, like a boy on Christmas morning, and we went down the back path along the river to a gravel bar and I shot for him. I drew and shot at pieces of bark he tossed upstream, as they floated past. I had him go against the bank behind me with his handkerchief and stick it against a tree. Then I had him come back beside me and say, "Turn," and I'd turn and shoot at it. I had him change it every time, side to side, up and down, always different, to show him what I meant by finding the target quick and nailing it dead. I was feeling better that morning and my shooting showed the results of a sound, long sleep and less liquor. It was almost fun—almost. It never can be that, never in a life like mine. Not when I thought about the past, and the present, and the almost inevitable end. But if it was ever pleasure, it was that day. I fired twenty-four shots, twelve from each gun, to show him what I could do with them. He watched and he saw the bullets go home true, with one near miss, and he still couldn't believe it.

Finally he said, "Can you do that with a rifle?"

"You mean, turning?" I asked.

"No," he said. "Can you shoot distance with a rifle?"

"Fair," I said. "Just fair. You can beat me with a rifle easy. I know that. I see it in your eyes. You're a rifle man. Me, I've never been where I needed a rifle." I looked at him then and added, "Maybe I ought to learn."

"Maybe you ought," he said slowly. "Maybe you could teach me your way and I'll show you mine."

Then I knew he was a good man with a rifle. When he talked about a rifle, his eyes started to shine. He knew, that was all, just as I knew my hand guns. And I was curious.

I said, "Who taught you rifle?"

"I'm lucky," he said gently. "I want you to meet him. He's an old man now, lives down the river in the Cup about fifteen miles. All by himself in a cabin. His name is Ronson. Sam Ronson. He's a mountain man. He's got a lot of rifles, but he still loves the oldest one. It was made by somebody named Farrell. It's a muzzle loader, tall as a tree. I been goin' down to see him 'most every week for three years.''

"Farrell," I said softly. "You got any idea who Farrell was?"

"Sam don't talk much," he said. "Least, about that Farrell. Once I asked something or other about who he was, and Sam sort of looked sideways with them bright gray eyes that look like he's ready to cry, and he just said, 'He was a man, son,' and that was all. I never did have the guts to ask him again."

"I'd like to know him," I said. "When can we pay him a visit?"

"So you might stick around?" he said.

I said, "Long enough to see him." It was too soon to commit myself,

"We'll go later this week," he said. "I got to take him some flour."

I reloaded and holstered my guns and turned up the path. He followed me to the bank and we stood for a moment, staring west toward the horizon. He grinned and said, "I'll see you tonight," and went south along the road with a hundred unanswered questions between us. I wanted to know him better. I wanted to call him Dan, wanted him to call me Jim. I hadn't felt that way about a man in years; it was a strange feeling and against my code, but this was a crazy deal.

She said, "That was wonderful shooting, Mr. Stanton."

I hadn't heard her come up. I wheeled, masking my surprise, and saw her step out of the trees along the bank. She'd been there all the time I shot for Dan. This was a full day, I thought, getting a visit from her father and now her.

I said, "Miss Bisonette, don't do that again."

She smiled and shoved her hands deep in her skirt pockets. She was sure of herself because of her father's money and his reputation. She said, "Why not?"

I said, "I remembered your voice, Miss Bisonette. Otherwise. . ." I didn't smile.

I didn't wait to see how she figured that out. I walked to the store and went inside, and she followed me. I saw her spring buggy in the shade on the west side of the store, with the matched bays stamping delicately on the ground, impatient to be off. It was one of those new rigs with striped wheels and cornucopian designs painted on the sides, probably their family crest. I wanted to ask a lot of questions about the Bisonette family. They had money, all right, to afford matched teams and fancy buggies and a bunch of hired men who had time to ride around on a work day.

She stood across the counter and watched me clean my guns. She was calm and smiling and altogether wise about this country of hers and how a man thought of his guns before himself. She wore different clothing today, a brown riding skirt and a short green jacket and a black, low-crowned hat with a braided leather band that ended in a fancy knot with the two smooth ends hanging over the hat brim. She was vivid and alive, and she watched me with great interest.

She said, "I won't call behind your back again, Mr. Stanton. I understand."

I looked up and smiled. I said, "Thanks."

"Well. . ." she said.

"Now tell my why you stopped, Miss Bisonette," I said. "Have you seen your father this afternoon?"

"Yes," she said. "That's why I'm here."

Now I was surprised. I said, "You saw him, and you came here?"

"I met him going home," she said. "I told him I'd stop and see you, and he thought it was a good idea."

"Your honesty is so painful I suspect it," I said. "And

why did he think it was such a good idea? Three hours ago he gave me one week to leave the country."

She laughed then, throwing her head back and showing me the long curving line of her neck and her fine white teeth. She said, "He didn't retract the week's grace, but he's always willing to settle a problem peaceably. We want to curry your favor, of course, to ask you to dinner some night, give you good cigars and decent liquor, a soft bed and a bath in a tub, and send you home thinking we're really wonderful people."

"You know," I said. "You're a remarkable woman, and so is your story. And after that?"

"Why," she smiled, "then we hope you reconsider about selling your property."

There had to be something behind her smile and her words. She was simply working a new twist with an old game. Instead of trying once and then shooting, they came out in the open—up to a point—and offered a truce and the breaking of bread, and to confuse me, told me exactly why they offered the willow branch. I wanted to like her, and couldn't make it a complete trust. But this was a challenge I had to meet.

"Miss Bisonette," I said, "you've been honest with me. I'll be the same. I came here to sell this store and ride on. When I saw it, I was afraid I wouldn't net the cost of my ride. Then everything happened. I'm not blind. I hear and see things and I smell a profit as well as other men. Something big is happening in this valley. Innocently, I'm on the chambered shell, looking through the slot at the cocked hammer. Common sense tells me to accept your father's excellent price. But I'm not a sensible man, never was, never will be. So I'll just stick around and see what happens. Do you blame me?"

"How long?" she said. "One week?"

"Time has no beginning or ending," I said. "I always drift with it."

She said, "No, I don't blame you. When shall we expect you to dinner?"

I said, "Well. . ." and had to cough. It was a bad spell and I grabbed my handkerchief and turned away, and she came around the counter and held my shoulders and said, "You're sick. You've got to see a doctor."

I swallowed and looked at her, and we stood that way for a moment, and then she stepped back and turned pink. She said, "You are sick. Admit it."

"This is Tuesday," I said. "Would Sunday be convenient?"

She said, "You're a stubborn fool. Yes, Sunday, by all means."

She went out to her buggy and drove west. I watched her go and looked at my handkerchief. It was spotted with red and I was going to dinner on Sunday, and time was running out. I saw dust on the hilltop, last sign of her buggy, and looked at the sun hanging just above her dust. It had never looked warmer to me. Maybe a man saw all things as beautiful when his life was a red stain between his hands, running out before his time. I locked the store and went back to sleep until night.

Hannigan and Mary came at eight that night and I let them in the kitchen door and blocked the window before we sat at the table. Hannigan was more subdued with her along, but not enough to conceal his eagerness for open talk. For her part, Mary Carr shook my hand strongly and said, "Won't you call me Mary? I'd like to call you Jim, and I know Dan would. He told me everything that happened today."

I liked her more every time she smiled or spoke. She was dressed in blue work pants and worn boots, with a faded green shirt tucked tight under her belt and her light

brown hair pushed up under her wrinkled black hat. She
wore a brown leather jacket, swinging open. On first look
she appeared shoddy, but the boots were fine-grained
leather and the shirt was that beautiful grade of cloth rarely
found this far west. Her father had had money, I decided,
and probably left her fairly well fixed. Somehow, I felt that
she was playing a temporary role, wearing the old, faded
clothing, waiting patiently for better days and a chance to
blossom out in the dresses she would wear like a queen. I
wondered if Dan realized this, and decided she was being
sensible, giving Dan a chance to make good and give her
all these things, rather than use any money her father had
left and make him feel bad from the start. Hannigan was
luckier than he knew, I decided that night, and I found
Mary presenting a stronger picture than Charlotte Bisonette, although they were entirely different and offered no
true comparison.

Mary made coffee while we talked, and after a few minutes of sparring Dan said, "I'm for telling you everything,
Jim. Mary, are you with me?"

Mary turned from the stove and said, "Of course, Dan.
I wouldn't have come tonight if I hadn't trusted Jim."

"When did you decide that?" I smiled.

She laughed softly. "When you told me to find the pepper and then accepted my price."

"Did you really need pepper?" I asked.

They looked at each other and smiled. Mary said, "No."

She poured the coffee which was immeasurably better
than my own, and they started talking. They talked and
talked, first one, then the other, each one adding points and
correcting the other at times. Unrolling before me was a
picture of this valley and the trouble in it, a complete picture to the limit of their knowledge, which was consider-
able. The story was this:

Until a year ago this country had been peaceful. There

were a few farmers on the east side of the river, the first homesteaders who always precede a rush. To the west, far out, Bisonette and a few other big ranchers had been in business about ten years, ever since the country became safe enough to exploit. Bisonette was the big man, the leader of the ranchers. Blackwater was only a trading post. Then the railroad started crawling northwest and everything changed.

Blackwater was on the direct route. Weeping Water boomed. Settlers were pouring into the country. Blackwater grew to three hundred people in a year. And out of nowhere came Mixon to organize the farmers who, by this summer, had taken all available land on the east side of the river. The railroad would reach Blackwater the next summer and that meant the opening of everything for this valley. All this, Mary and Dan said, seemed to be at the bottom of the trouble.

Bisonette and the ranchers didn't want farmers creeping over on the west bank. They couldn't do anything about the three landowners already there—Simpson, Dan and Mary's father—but they were making certain no one else came over. Simpson was a Bisonette man, had opened his store with a loan from Bisonette, and supplied the ranchers; but Dan was nobody's man and Mary's father had refused to sell to either side when the trouble started. Then, almost a year ago, Mary's father had disappeared and never turned up. But Mary stayed right on the farm and Dan helped her, and they both refused to sell.

I said it didn't make sense, fighting each other when the railroad would benefit both factions. Bisonette and the ranchers would have a straight cattle haul to market and save a long drive to a distant railroad. The farmers would have the same advantage for their products. Everything, in turn, would be shipped in cheaper for the valley. What difference could three quarter sections of land make in such a big deal?

Mary offered her explanation. Bisonette was a proud man, a kind of king on his land. And he owned it, too; he wasn't just exercising the right of eminent domain. He'd had his men homestead it in the beginning and when they proved up, he bought it from them. The other ranchers had done the same during the past years. They owned outright all the land from the west bank of the river, so far west it didn't make much difference where they stopped because out that far the land was only good for range anyway. So it wasn't a question of losing free grass, nor was it a bigger question.

That was the railroad getting free grants for building through. The government had opened this country to homestead before the railroad company decided to build, and instead of getting thousands of acres on both sides of the track for building, as did other lines only short years before, the railroad had to buy right-of-way from the landowners and pay a fair price. Of course, no one could hold the railroad up because the government could force a sale, so Bisonette and the other ranchers had long ago agreed to sell all the land necessary for the construction. That just made good sense, Mary said, and Bisonette had never been accused of being stupid. Nor was Mixon and his Granger organization. They agreed wholeheartedly.

And still the fight was on, and coming to a climax. I could see that. They both knew it. In fact, Dan told me that Simpson would have sold to Bisonette long before, had Bisonette wanted to close the deal. And then Mixon came along and scared the living hell out of Simpson, until he didn't know what to do. Dan told us he would bet Simpson held out plenty of cash and wanted to lose that title and clear out. And when I thought back, I began to wonder.

So here we were, the three of us, with three little quarter

sections battling both sides in something I began to understand, and then, thinking it over, could not understand.

I said, finally. "It might be this: they both figure the town will boom and our land will be worth a fortune split into lots."

"No," Mary said. "Two miles is so far south the town wouldn't grow this far in our lifetime. You know that, Jim."

I had to agree with her; that was true. I said, "All right, you've told me plenty, but not enough. Something else is behind this deal. I want to know what it is. I'll stay right here until I find out. Will you stick with me? I'm for you, both of you. I want to see you—" I grinned and they both blushed—"married and happy."

"I'm with you," Dan said.

"Of course," Mary smiled. "But we can't sleep a minute, Jim. We've got to watch them all the time." She frowned. "So far, except for Father's—well, there has been no shooting. I'm afraid that day is almost done."

"So?" I said.

"So we'll fight," Mary said firmly. "All of us, if we have to, until this is cleared up."

Dan said, "I think we better visit Sam tomorrow."

"Fine," I said. "I want to meet him."

It was getting late and we stopped talk for the night. Mary looked at me sharply before they went out, and said, "Jim, will you see Charles Nichols for me?"

"Who's he?" I asked.

Dan said, "He's a doctor. He's everything, Jim. He lives in town."

"Got a license?" I asked. "Too many doctors out here are self-styled."

Mary said, "Let him tell you, Jim. I want him to examine you. Will you do it?"

Two women in one day were worried about my health.

I was too tired to argue. I said, "Yes, Mary. Soon as I can. Now you two head for home. Dan, have you got an extra horse?"

"I'll bring him along," Dan said. "Before sunup. You be ready."

I said good night and they started outside. The shot lanced from up the road toward town. Mary fell and Dan caught her and dropped beside her. I jumped outside and slammed the kitchen door, cutting off the shooter's light. I said, "Hold her, Dan," and bent down to find the wound. She whispered, "Keep down, I'm all right."

She wasn't hit; just playing it smart and thinking faster than most women ever would. Dan said, "You all right, Mary?"

"Yes," she said. "Did you see where the shot came from?"

"Up there," Dan said, "And no use looking tonight. Too close to town and the river."

"That's twice," I said. "They knew Mary was here. Shooting at a woman. The joke is all finished. We'll find that slug in the morning, Dan, and start a little hell raising on our own."

Mary said, "Don't be hasty, Jim."

"Hasty," I said. "They miss you by two inches and you tell me to sleep it off and forgive everybody in the morning. Dan, you take Mary home and make sure she's safe."

I squatted beside the door while Dan led her along the back wall and through the trees that flanked the road. Far off I heard muffled sounds—a horse trotting with hoofs sacked. I made a slow and cautious circle of the store, stood for half an hour in the trees along the river, and then went to bed. Tomorrow would be a nice day, I thought, better than the one just passed.

Three

I FELT BETTER THE NEXT MORNING. I WASHED AND THEN followed an impulse and unpacked my valise, ignored the whisky flask, and changed clothes. I dressed in a pair of loose corduroy trousers and a pair of soft calfskin walking boots with thick soles and flat heels and comfortable wide toes. I slipped into a brown wool shirt that fitted me snugly, adjusted and placed my holsters and guns, and put on a travel-wrinkled tweed coat, fuzzy and rough and smelling of tobacco. The coat hung baggy and loose, covering my guns and giving me plenty of room for a smooth draw. I wadded the black suit and the stiff white shirt into a ball and stuffed them into the valise; and somehow, taking off the traditional clothes that marked a gambler like a brand on each cheek, and dressing in old clothes, made me feel different. I wondered if a man could shed the past as easily as he changed clothes; push one life into the bottom of his valise and put on another that fitted not so tight and profitable, perhaps, but a lot smoother on his conscience. I pushed the valise under the bed and went out to cook breakfast.

I finished as gray dawn was tinting the kitchen window, and taking a butcher knife, went outside and searched for the slug. It had struck ten feet up, embedding itself in the trimmed log plate. I got a rickety ladder and climbed up and dug it out. Inside, washing it off and weighing it in my hand, I couldn't tell the caliber because it was smashed shapeless, but it felt like a .45-.70. So much for that, I thought, now for the owner. I heard horses and went outside as Dan galloped up from the south, leading a roan.

"Climb up," he said. "You look better this morning, Jim."

"Good sleep," I said. "I've got the slug."

I hadn't ridden for two years but I swung on the roan and felt him tense and gauge me, and then stand loose-legged, nuzzling Dan's big bay. Dan said, "What caliber?"

".45-.70, maybe," I said. "Let's ride to town."

"Sure," Dan said. "We can make old Sam's later on today. .45-.70, huh? Not so many of them guns around. We'll ask the marshal—not that it'll do any good—and then see Doc."

"Was Mary all right?" I asked.

We swung from the yard and headed for town, the road moving smoothly under me. Dan said, "She's all right, Jim," and glanced at me, and said, "You rode lately?"

"I'll be split to the neck by night," I said. "Even on a fat-backed plowhorse."

We passed Mary's place on the ride to town, a small frame house and sod outbuildings, and dismounted in front of the Levy Mercantile Company, in front of which, two days ago, Mixon had knocked Bisonette into the dust and started me on the endless trail of trouble. People watched us get down and tie the horses and stand together on the warped boardwalk; and I wondered if someone along this street was looking at us and cursing himself for shooting high on a dark night.

"Here comes the marshal," Dan said. "Name's Brent."

I'd been wondering about the law in this town. I was certain they had a village marshal because Weeping Water was the county seat and its sheriff would have his hands full in that town alone. But where, I thought, had the marshal been hiding when Mixon knocked Bisonette down?

"Whose man?" I asked, watching Brent come up the sidewalk.

"Mixon's man," Dan said. "Voted in last fall. He's just what he looks."

Brent was a lanky, slightly stooped man who walked with that peculiar plunging gait of the horseman who hated to walk across the street. He wore plain brown pants and a blue shirt, with a sagging, black, sateen-backed vest, his star pinned on the top vest pocket over his heart, and tobacco sack and papers sticking above the star. He looked lazy and dirty and harmless, if you stopped at his belly, or missed his eyes. Then he came nearer and I saw them, yellowish-green, sharp and inquisitive under heavy lids and bushy brows. He wore two gun belts which canted snugly on each hip and were tied down, and his guns were well-worn .44s with faded brown-bone handles. It's a funny thing about men wearing two guns like that; most of them are trying to put on a front and make people believe they are the devil's own son. And then you see a few men who wear two guns and aren't putting on any front and don't tell you what they can do, and you know they can handle those guns. That was Brent.

He came abreast of us and said, "Howdy, Dan."

"Mornin', Brent," Dan said. "This is Jim Stanton."

Brent made no move to shake hands. He said, "Heard of you, Stanton."

I said, "Can't say the same, Brent."

He showed no resentment in his body; only his eyes opened a little and studied me. He said, "What's on your mind, Dan?"

Dan said, "I want to buy a .45-.70. Who packs 'em around here?"

Brent rubbed a long, soiled thumb against his flabby nose and said, "Can't think of nobody right off, Dan. I'll ask around."

Dan said, "I'd appreciate it. Come on, Jim. Let's get them pills."

Brent watched us cross the street, I know, because he didn't move when we turned away. He was no more a town marshal than I was a choir boy. And I knew where he'd been two days ago—out of town conveniently while Mixon made his tough play with Bisonette. He'd come up the trail from Texas, that was a cinch, and no marshal in a town this size was ever like him, or needed to be. He looked sleepy and he was dangerous as a rattler on a hot day in a rock quarry. He was a dirty, unkempt man personally, but his gun belts and holsters were oiled every day, and those brown-handled .44s were clean as mountain spring water. I had known other men like him in the trail towns, on the West Coast, and through the Southwest but not here. He spelled trouble and his eyes capitalized every letter of the word. I put him directly under Mixon on my list; and there only because Mixon had the brain and Brent lived by instinct.

I said, "He killed anybody here?"

"One," Dan said. "Last fall. Fella from Weeping Water. They had trouble in a card game and went out in the street. Fella never got his gun level. That was before election."

"So," I said. "Where's this Nichols' place?"

"Lift your eyes," Dan said, "or it'll hit you right in the nose."

Nichols' so-called drugstore was a two-storied frame building on the west side of Main in the middle of the business block; and the strange thing about it was, I felt that it had been there a long time and belonged. Yet it was barely a year old. Wind and weather had beaten the un-painted outside to a grayish-brown and the two benches flanking the door were carved with initials and tilted a little drunkenly against the store front. It had one fairly large window on the left of the door, and in this window was a stuffed skunk on a flat pedestal, flanked by two five-gallon bottles of colored water, one red, the other green.

Dan pushed the door back and we stepped into the drug-store, hearing the bell jingle in the rear. I looked around closely for signs of those things in the store which would be directly reflected in the man. The floor was spotless, that front window was shining, the walls and ceiling were plastered and painted a light blue; and the smell was won-derful. It was a combination of drugs and soda flavoring and herbs and fine tobacco. Of all things to find in this little town, a soda fountain was on the right with the fla-voring jars sticking their different colored tops above the marble top and labeled, "Lemon, Raspberry, Strawberry" and one that said, "God knows," which I took for a mix-ture of all. On down from the soda fountain was a prescrip-tion case with a big mortar and pestle, the bottles on shelves against the wall, each gold-labeled with the name of its drug. Across the store was a long counter from window to the door in back, and behind this counter, on shelves, was the most mixed, conglomerate assortment of patent medi-cines, stationery, cigar boxes, pipes on display boards, but-tons, needles, everything under the sun you didn't expect; and high on the wall above this mess of man's pottage that was certainly safe from anybody's birthright a big sign said: "Help yourself—not responsible for the results."

Dan bawled, "Doc—hey, Doc!"

"All right, all right," a deep voice called. "Keep your shirt on."

Charles Nichols came from the rear of his drugstore and

stopped before me; and I liked this man without a word or
a handshake. He was middle-aged and short, and round as
one of those bulbous brandy barrels from France. His eyes
were dark brown and his nose was short in the middle of
a broad, plump face, with a tremendous dragoon mustache
covering his upper lip and sweeping magnificently down
each side of his jaw, which was square and looked as solid
as granite. He wore a suit of greenish nankeen with a
starched white shirt, and round-toed Texas boots with gold
stitching. His hands were the finest part of the man; long
and wide and clean, with slender delicate fingertips. I never
saw dirt under his fingernails; I never saw dirt on him. He
was an odd-looking little figure of a man, but his face and
eyes and hands were good. I could see something of myself
in this man; and that sounds foolish, but it was true.

"Doc," Dan said. "This is Jim Stanton."

Doc Nichols shook my hand firmly and said, "I thought
you were a gambler?"

"Clothes change a man," I said. "I took them off this
morning."

"Well," Doc said. "Nobody'd ever know you were a
gambler in those duds unless he noticed your fingers and
the ring and your hair and your guns and those red spots
on your cheeks. And all of your face, mostly your eyes.
Come on back and have a sarsaparilla."

I said, "You need glasses, Doc," and we all laughed.

He didn't see much, oh no, not him. Just every fly on
that Main Street and how the wind rolled individual tum-
bleweeds along the ridges ten miles north of town. Here
was a little man who looked like a dude, on first glance,
and a lot more every glance after that.

Doc said, "I've heard about you, Jim. Mary told me
some, Dan helped out in his tongue-tied way, and Charlotte sort of raked you over the hot coals yesterday noon."

"So?" I said.

"So I'd like you to know something," Doc said, when we were settled in his small back room under the stairs. "I'm neutral in this town but I hate a coward and a liar. Everybody tells me their troubles. I've got a few special friends and no enemies. No enemies, mostly, because they're afraid they might get sick and I'd cut their liver out and feed it to them before they recognized their own bile. I came out here two years ago for peace and quiet. I was the twenty-first resident of this metropolis. Now look at it!" Doc grimaced and took a deep gulp of sarsaparilla. "Something's going on. It looks simple and it isn't. You ought to know. You seem to have a talent for making enemies."

"Have you formed an opinion?" I asked.

"Yes," Doc said. "I'll keep it to myself. In the meantime, let's take a look at you."

I said, "Now hold on. I didn't come. . ."

Dan grinned and grabbed my arms and said, "Calm down, you fire-eater. Doc's gonna examine you if I have to sit on you."

I smiled at them. No use arguing with these people. I said, "All right, Dan. I won't run. But it's foolish, Doc. I'm just run-down."

Doc said, "Take off your coat and shirt, Jim. We'll have a look."

I peeled off, handed my guns and holsters to Dan, and Doc walked around me and tapped my back and chest and stomach, and grunted meaningless words to himself. He took my pulse and looked in my ears and pulled out a big white handkerchief and started to blow his nose and suddenly slapped my back. I coughed and he had that handkerchief against my mouth and away before I knew what he'd done. He looked at the flecks of blood on the white linen, and stared at my face and my chest.

He said, "Jim, how long has this been going on?"

"A few months," I said. "It doesn't bother me."

His eyes glared at me. He said, "You damned fool! Are you deliberately trying to kill yourself? You know you've got consumption, or that's what they call it these days. I call it lung fever, the worst kind, and you've let yourself go a long time."

Dan murmured, "I thought so," and I looked at them and knew it was no use lying to Jim Stanton any longer. I had it bad, and I'd been too stubborn to do something about it. I said, "What do you want me to do, Doc? Go to bed? Drink milk? Live like a spinster?"

"Please," Doc said softly. "Let's not joke about this, Jim. If you don't do something for yourself, you'll be dead in a year. That I can promise. Neither can I tell you the way to health. But I can tell you how to get some strength back and maybe fight it off from this dangerous stage. If you want to try?"

I wondered how long I would be in Blackwater; how long to help Dan and Mary win the happiness they deserved. I said, "Tell me what to do, Doc. I'll try. But understand—I've got a few things to do and they come first."

He understood. He said, "Fine. Now I can't tell you much because nobody knows a lot about this disease. But I know this: a high, dry climate helps. No drinking. Plenty of sleep. The less excitement, the better. Lots of milk. Cut out smoking cigars. Regular exercise. And peace of mind."

I laughed at him. I couldn't help it. I said, "According to that, Doc, I don't know it, but I'm dead already. I can try some of those, but the others will have to wait a little. I'll stop drinking and smoking. I'll try to get a lot of sleep. You've got some altitude here, about two thousand, I'd say, but not enough. Maybe I'll take a trip to Santa Fe in a few weeks. What do you say to that?"

"Fair enough," Doc said. "Now let's talk about rifles."

"And land," I said. "And cattlemen and farmers and a few other things."

The bell tinkled and Doc went out and mixed up a soda for a boy and gave him strict orders to drink it slow, and then came back and said, "You get dressed, Jim. Might catch cold. Now where would you like to begin this discussion of land and such—with the countour farming of the Chinese?"

An hour later Dan and I went down to the general store and got Sam's flour and tied the sack to his saddle.

I didn't know a great deal more about the situation than the night before, but I had points clarified and people brought into remorseless light by Doc's sharp tongue. But this was part of it: the slug was a .45-.70 and several people owned them, including Higgens, who was now living with a friend on the north side of town. Higgens spent his days in the Big H, drinking and playing cards and talking with those men who cared for his company; no one seemed to know what he did at night except sleep. That was one thing. I had the history of Bisonette, of Mixon, of all the people involved. Bisonette had been in this country ten years, coming from Texas with a big trail herd and settling down, to be followed by the other ranchers living near him. Mixon was supposed to be from Chicago and before that from God knows where. He came along and organized the farmers before anyone knew his purpose; and then his friends started to drift in, and his organization grew as more settlers bought land and built their places. Mary Carr and her father came from Ohio; this was told by both Dan and Doc, as a matter of explaining about her. John Carr refused to sell his farm, as Dan had told me before, and had disappeared completely not quite a year ago. No one had found a trace of his body. Mary stayed on the farm, and Dan helped her, and she hired a man in the spring and fall for her heavy work. She had enough money and seemed to get along very well. Dan told me about himself when Doc brought fresh glasses of raspberry soda for a farewell drink. Dan's father came from Kentucky and had been one of the last Mountain Men, the trappers who opened up the West. He met a girl in Westport, was married, and spent the next few years between his home and the mountains, but mostly in the mountains. Dan was the only result of this fleeting union, for his father went out one year and never came back. His mother died just before the war, and Dan was first a drummer boy and then a bugler in a St. Louis Company that fought under Grant along the Mississippi. Dan came west on a river boat after the war, bought his farm from a New Englander who wanted to go home to his stone pastures, met old Sam who had known his father, and settled down to stay at least a few years.

We untied the horses and ducked under the rail to mount when I saw Mixon standing on the sidewalk. He was alone and he held up his hand and said, "Stanton, got a minute?"

I said, "Speak up, Mixon. Just a minute."

"I'm sorry about the other day," Mixon said. "I got off half-cocked."

"You sure did," Dan said evenly.

"Hannigan," Mixon said coldly. "Don't get me wrong. We'll get together one of these days, and that's a promise."

"Fine," Dan said. "The sooner the better."

Mixon turned to me again, unruffled, and said, "Could I see you again, about this business?"

It wouldn't make any difference, I thought, and Mixon wasn't a man to shoot people in the back. For all his doubtful traits, I had to respect him. I said, "Any time, Mixon."

"That's decent of you," he said. "I'd like to ride out tonight."

"Before dark," Dan said.

"I'm asking Stanton," Mixon said softly. "Name your time, Stanton."

"Make it morning," I said, thinking of the ride ahead. "Sunrise."

Mixon said, "I'll be there," and walked up the street. I watched him while I mounted, and when we rode south on the way to Sam Ronson's, Dan smiled and said, "You've got him worried, Jim."

"And you?" I asked.

"He's been talking around for a year," Dan said. "Maybe he'll want to stop talking and try a little action in the morning." He looked at me. "After you talk with him. Maybe he won't feel like talking if I get to him first."

"Don't misjudge him," I said. "Now let's ride before I bust in two."

We rode south, passing Mary's and the store, and pulled in for a drink of water at Dan's, one mile south of the store. I had wondered whether his home was neat and clean, or the rat nest most men seem to build around them when they live alone. When I turned down the lane and saw the sod walls and the shingled roof, the well-kept yard, and the barn next to the river, I knew Dan was a clean man in his own home. His cabin was one big room with a lean-to kitchen on the rear and a big fireplace built into the north wall. The plank floor was scrubbed nearly white and his pots and pans and dishes were hung and stacked in neat piles and rows in the kitchen. He had laid full round beech logs across the sod walls, and smaller round logs for rafters and cross braces; and from these bare braces hung bunches of onions and a tuft of dry sage and a string of carrots tied by their tops.

We drank at the well and I said, "You'd make a good wife, Dan," and he blushed and threw a dipperful at me and said, "Ah, a man's got to smell his own house. I don't like dirt."

We rode on to the south and left the Weeping Water road at the lower ford, to ride then on a narrower trail which soon dropped us between the closing, climbing hills thick with cottonwoods and willows and beeches, growing thickly along the river and towering like ancient kings above the stunted jack pines and little willows and plum brush matted around their trunks. It was fifteen miles down-river to Sam Ronson's place and the farther south we rode, the wilder it got.

The valley narrowed to a canyon in less than three miles' riding, and I saw that the wide, fertile valley behind was a freak of nature, like a sport dog, happening through some quirk of Mother Earth's upheavals and settling. Dan explained that the valley was about twenty miles long, starting at his place five miles south of town and extending some fifteen miles north beyond the town. But here, with a quick reversal of form, was wild country, bottom country, filled with thickets and small, clay sided ravines and canyons running into the river, each having its own creek or spring that added another water trickle to the river and made it, when it swung to the east and passed Weeping Water, the wide, deep channel I had seen from the train. This country was too rough for farming, too wild for profitable cattle raising; it was a short belt of wilderness extended twenty miles north and south, and some ten east and west. No one wanted it; no one fought over it; and Sam Ronson lived in the middle and loved the life.

Dan told me that old Sam had to leave his beloved mountains and drop down to warmer, lower land because of his wounds which started acting up on him and giving him aches and pains all winter long; and Sam remembered this place and came to it eight years ago and built his house on the river and settled down to live out his years. He met

Dan and they got on well together, Dan explained, and Sam taught him how to shoot and hunt and trap, a thousand things, and Dan carried in his supplies and news of the outside world.

"He was fit to be tied," Dan said, "when I told him about the railroad coming. He was going out to fight 'em off by himself. But he scouted out and saw where they wouldn't come through the Cup, so he stopped worrying."

"What did you call this canyon?" I asked.

We had dropped lower and rode now between high walls of colored strata, and the river was compressed narrowly and running deep, giving off a thick hum. Dan said, "They call this middle part the 'Devil's Cup.' The name sort of spread until they call the whole business that."

We rounded a sharp turn in the narrow trail that followed the river and I saw a combination of log-and-sod house set back from the bank on our side, shaded by the canyon wall and surrounded by trees that moved their upper branches in the wind and threw dancing shadows on the roof and the bare head of the old man sitting beside the open door. I saw a low stable behind the house and a path leading down to a short log dock extending a few feet into the river. A flat-bottomed skiff was tied to the dock, and on wooden horses near the dock was a long canoe, bottom up, gleaming wetly from recent painting. But it was the old man who dominated this scene. The trees and the canyon were beautiful, and the birds and water and wind made sweet music, but the old man drew my glance from nature.

Dan called, "Ho, Sam!" and waved.

He sat motionless until we dismounted and stood before him. Then he rose and said, "Howdy, Dan," and looked at me.

"This is Jim Stanton," Dan said.

Sam Ronson's shake was like a snapping beaver trap. His eyes were an eagle's, set deep and bright in a thin, wrinkled face that held a hatchet sharpness through the long nose and heavy eyebrows, and outthrust, scarred jaw. He was an old man who carried his uncounted years like cottonwood fluff on his shoulders. He didn't weigh over a hundred and thirty pounds but that was all bone and muscle, and he stood straight and alert on his feet. He wore a blue shirt, tail out over brown blanket pants, slit at the bottoms. His feet were big and loose in a pair of beaded moccasins, and his hair was snow white and flowing like a waterfall behind his ears and down to his shoulders.

"Come in and set," he said. "You bring that flour, Dan?"

Dan took the sack from his saddle and carried it into the cabin. He said, "Fifty pounds, Sam. Enough for a spell."

"Empire State," Sam read the name on the sack. "No-count flour. Set it in the corner."

I looked around his cabin and found it plain and neat. He had plastered over the logs with a home-made mixture of mud and sand; and in the sod storeroom he had plastered over the sods and painted the smooth wall brown. His home was in this one big room with the storeroom connected by a wide door. The fireplace covered the entire south end of the cabin. His bed, two big tables, four chairs, and some big boxes, all handmade, comprised his furniture, not counting his cooking pots and dishes on a shelf beside the fireplace. The floor was split beech, shaved and sanded, polished in its natural color by his feet. The walls were stuck full of pegs, on which hung a wonderful variety of strange objects; it took me an hour to inspect them with my eyes while we talked.

Dan told him about me, sparing no details, not even my health, until I felt like a mouse under a cat's paw when he finished. Then Dan told about the happenings of the past two days, not going back more, for it was plain Sam knew all about the fight for the store and the three farms. He listened quietly, sitting at the big table, and when Dan finished, he was silent for fully a minute. Then he said, "I knew this was comin'. I don't plainly see why they want your store, Jim, or Dan's place, or the girl's. There's something behind this. Find it and let me know. Mebbe we can do a bit about it."

I said, "We'll do that, Sam. But I don't want to push my trouble on you."

He gave me a small, flinty smile. "Trouble, Jim? I'll tell you when it looks like bad trouble. Then I'll worry a little."

He was a fearless old man from another age I would never know, and I wondered what stories he could tell, if he would, about his years in the mountains. I wanted to ask him a thousand questions, and didn't know where to start. I looked at the long rifle above the fireplace and decided that was the best way.

"I'd love to see your rifles, Sam." I said.

It was dark when we stopped long enough to cook a meal. I had been privileged to hear through the simple words of an old man, unpretentious and matter-of-fact, the story of my country's advance to the Pacific; and when I considered that the Mountain Men had spearheaded that greatest of all movements only short years before, in the span of this old man's mature life, it gave me a strange feeling sitting, all at once, in the presence of the past, the present, and a good share of the future. And when I remembered the world I knew with its so-called great men, the bumblers and connivers, stupid officials, I was ashamed. For here was truly a great man who had done what those men talked about, who with his friends had opened all the land over which those *nouveau* great were now striding and taking credit for the conquering. Here was an old man living alone with his memories, with enough true history at his tongue tip to change maps and rewrite the gaudy, false pages of our history books over the period of an entire generation.

We talked of guns that afternoon, of hunting and fishing and fighting, of the mountains and the Pacific coast, of the war, the Indian campaigns, of everything that came to our minds. He showed me his long rifle and his other guns and told me about them, and he asked about my guns and when Dan praised my shooting until my ears turned red, we went outside and shot for an hour, and he said something everyone should remember, "A man's never too old to learn something." He was just as eager to learn my way of shooting, as I was to know his. I wish I could tell of all the things he told me that afternoon, but it would be better to only sketch all of them rather than elaborate because no one could remember everything in such a short space of time.

I had long been curious about those old long rifles, and he told me their story that afternoon. I held his rifle on my knees while he told its history. Farrell was the gunsmith who invented the grooved barrel, or so Sam had been told, and his rifle was one made by Farrell. It weighed about nine pounds and had a three-and-a-half-foot octagon barrel set into a stock of polished curly maple. The trigger guard was small and the hickory ramrod was held in place by brass rings beneath the barrel. Sam explained that originally it had been a flintlock but he had a gunsmith named Hawkins in St. Louis change it over for caps because priming powder got wet easily and wind could blow the pan clean. This was also the first rifle in which a greased linen patch was used to seat and hold the ball, and the balls were smaller and ran around fifty-two to a pound. This was the rifle that opened the mountains to men like Sam, and I knew it had served them well; it was not marred with those signs of a foolish man's vanity—notches—but I wondered how many could be inscribed if this old man would talk.

He shot for us, loading with such smoothness I missed the speed of his movements the first few times; and at distances up to a hundred yards, he broke small wood blocks and other objects at will. He admitted that beyond a range of two hundred yards, the old rifle was not too effective; but I thought of the newer rifles and how they shot, and it seemed to me their only advantage was greater speed.

He made me draw and shoot as I had for Dan the day before, and he watched a dozen shots in thin-lipped silence and then screeched like a cougar and cracked his heels in the air and clapped my back, saying, "That shines, Jim. That shines!" The way he said it, it meant more than winning a ten-thousand-dollar pot.

He showed me how he threw a knife, and he tried my shoulder draw and surprised me with his quickness. I tried his long rifle but I wasn't so good, and Dan then showed me that he was close to the old man with his own rifle. And after that we did so many things and talked so long that, as I said, my head was ringing with the stories at supper.

How to trap beaver; the way mountains look in winter; Blackfoot on the march; the Green River; Brown's Hole; the passes through the last mountains to California; Santa Fe in the days of the Spanish; Jim Bridger and Kit Carson and the Mountain Men; Fremont, and the less said about him, the better; how to tan a deerskin; how to press and pack beaver skins; the price of a skin; possible punches; the way the sky looks after a rain in the Jackson Hole country of Wyoming; the feel of dust crossing the Cimarron Desert, gritty and fine as ground glass on a man's mouth; loading and firing on the run; from a horse; the trees of Oregon and the redwoods of California; the way to let horses down a sheer drop with a pair of ropes. . . .But why go on? The more I remembered, the worse I felt to think I had been born too late to do and see the things Sam had lived.

Dan led our horses behind the cabin to the stable, fed them, and brought wood for the fire. We ate slowly and then sat before the fire and I watched them smoke and remembered Doc's words. Sam told me about one of their friends who got the lung fever and went to Santa Fe and got well. So I decided not to smoke for a while, at least until I gave Doc's prescription a fair chance. We went to bed early and I remembered nothing until Dan touched my shoulder and said, "Time to start, Jim."

It was long before sunrise but Sam had coffee and bacon and biscuits ready. We ate quickly and went out to the horses, and my legs rebelled. I was stiff all over and a little raw, to tell the truth. I shook hands with Sam and we mounted and swung north on the trail.

Sam said, "I'll be waitin for news, young 'uns."

Dan called, "You'll get it, Sam."

That was all. No fancy good-byes. We rode into the trees and the last I saw, turning in the saddle, was the old man walking toward the river, straight as a string, white hair shining even in the false dawn light and the river mist.

I said, "There's a man, Dan."

"No better," Dan said gently. "If we need a good man, we can't do better, no matter the age."

We came to Dan's farm, just before sunrise. Dan had to do his chores and look at a duck about to become a mother, and I rode on to the store alone. I dismounted, feeling the stiffness even in my ears, and tied the roan to a tree and opened the store. I didn't expect business. I wanted to get some fresh air inside and make it smell like a decent place instead of the pigsty Higgens had been running. I came through the store after opening the kitchen door and the back windows, and saw Mixon ride up and cross the yard to the front door. He was alone, and for this I had to respect him.

He ducked through the door and nodded to me. "Up early, Stanton."

"You're on time," I said. "What sort of talk are you planning?"

He pulled out a chair and straddled it, leaning his big arms on the chair back, and spoke slowly: "I don't know if Bisonette's been here since the other day, but I'd like to tell you my side of this business."

"He hasn't come back," I said. "Go to it."

"I can't tell you much you don't know," Mixon said. "Hannigan and Mary Carr should know the whole of it. And Doc Nichols, too." He grinned. "Small town, news travels fast."

"You can leave Doc out," I said. "He's taking no sides."

"Sure," Mixon said. "No offense to Doc. He's a fine man. But you know why we want this land, Stanton. And Hannigan's and Mary Carr's."

"Do I?" I said.

"Hell," Mixon said shortly. "We want a foothold on this side of the river. Bisonette's been lording it over this valley long enough. Running cattle on fine farm land"— Mixon snorted—"and me with a hundred families waiting back east to get in, with money to buy that land. I could place over a hundred of 'em on this valley land Bisonette and the other ranchers use to fatten a few cows. Do you see my point?"

"If you did get this land," I said, "then what? It's only a drop in the bucket."

"That's our worry," Mixon said. "We'll take care of that. What I can't understand is you holding this when we bid it to ten times its value. I mean, to either of us. What's your reason, Stanton?''

He was really serious; he knew the life behind me because he'd been over that trail himself, and my stand didn't make sense to him. It hadn't made sense to me two days ago, but it did now. But I couldn't tell him why; I couldn't tell myself, in words. There was more to it, of course than wanting a foothold on this side. But that was the unknown I had to figure out, and that would take time. The reason I couldn't put it in words was something inside me, and that was my secret. For Mixon, for Bisonette, the apparent reasons were enough.

"You know why," I said evenly. "There's another reason behind all these offers. You know it; Bisonette knows it; but that's as far as it goes. Now it might mean nothing to me, and again, it could mean a great deal. I'm referring to money, Mixon. When one of you, or both, come over and tell me what it is, or I dig it up myself, then I'll do my figuring and decide to sell or hold. Why don't you admit I'm right? We talk the same language, Mixon. Only we're on different streets.''

He was losing his temper in big chunks. He got up and clenched his fists and scraped his boots on the floor. He said, "All right, Stanton. You don't make sense and you can't make any money in this country. Bisonette gave you a week to leave the country. I'll match that. After that . . .'' he just looked at me and smiled without humor.

"That's fine," I said. "That's the way I like things. I'd hate to have Bisonette scare me so bad and have you playing second fiddle to him. Now we can all lean back and take a deep breath and stop the baby games.''

"You want it," Mixon said. "You'll get it.''

I laughed at him. "In the back?''

"From me?" he said. "No, Stanton. Not from me. You'll know where it comes from when you get it. It's too bad you aren't man size. I'd enjoy breaking your neck with my bare hands.''

"That's a shame." I said softly. ''It's too bad you aren't man size with that gun you left behind this morning, just to show me you weren't hunting trouble, or was that the reason?''

That got him. He turned red and took a step for me, and then stopped. I piled it on. I said, ''But that's all right, Mixon. You've always got those two bums and the marshal to do that work for you.''

"Brent would like nothing better," he said. "You're just another frock coat to him, Stanton.''

I had gauged his marshal. I knew Brent's kind. Fast with a gun, yes, but not in my class. I wasn't bragging. None of them had ever seen me draw as I could; none of them would unless it had to be for keeps. Then they would know; but Brent would only have about half a second to see it. After that it wouldn't make any difference to him, ever.

I said, "Talk is foolish, Mixon. The week is up in five days, isn't it? Do we declare a truce till then, or is your business running out of time?''

"Till then," Mixon said. "You've got my promise. I'll keep it." He swore at the ground and said again, "I'd like to break your neck. . .''

"Start on me," Dan said from the door.

He had walked up from his place for the roan. We hadn't heard him until he stood in the door. Mixon turned and Dan said again, "Start on me, Mixon. Come on out. We got plenty of room. You've been bragging for a year now. Come on out!''

Mixon verified my thought about his courage. And watching him stare at Dan, stand quietly for a moment, and then start for the door, I wondered if Dan's greater size and strength was enough. Mixon had the walk and look of a man who knew his fists and his ring work. He would bring a bagful of dirty fighting tricks against Dan's strength, and it might not be a pretty thing to watch. But I couldn't stop them; and I didn't want to.

I followed them into the yard and said, "How do you want this to go?"

Dan said, "Why, just fight, that's all."

"How about knockdowns?" I said. "Do you let the man get up?"

Mixon said, "The hell with that Queensberry stuff. We'll fight, Stanton. We'll fight till one of us is done. That go with you, Hannigan?"

"Why sure," Dan said softly. "Jim, you kinda keep watch."

"It's your party," I said. "But one thing. When a man is down, there'll be no boots on him. If I think one of you is out, I'll tell the other. And that one will stand back. I'll revive that man. If he wants to go on, you'll go on. Otherwise, it's a fight. Got that?"

Mixon just grunted. I said, "You hear me, Mixon! You listen to me if that happens, or I blow your legs off."

That made him find his tongue. He said, "All right, Stanton. Let's get on."

I leaned against the store and said, "Go to it!"

What an inadequate manner to start the greatest fight I ever saw. When I thought of the ring matches I'd seen, good money paid for the dubious privilege, and compared them with this fight, it was like placing the moon beside the sun.

They moved in on each other, stripped from the waist up, both of them in bare feet after I told them no boots; and this was my first chance to compare them. They were a match when I considered the attributes of each. Dan weighed at least two-seventy and towered five inches over Mixon and had a longer reach. Mixon was six-two and weighed about two-forty, and was thicker-chested and heavier-legged than Dan. Mixon was my age, I judged, maybe a year or two older. And he wasn't fat. He was hard, like Dan, and they were an awe-inspiring sight moving for each other. I didn't know if Dan had anything but his strength and lasting power, but I knew Mixon had the tricks. This was the test; all I could do was stand and watch.

They were three feet apart and Dan reached one long arm out, open-palmed, and slapped Mixon's face with more power than I had in a full fist blow. Dan laughed then, as Mixon's head snapped back, and said, "Come on! Show me all those tricks."

Mixon wouldn't be bluffed into a blind rage. He tucked his jaw into his shoulder and bored in. Dan stood his ground. They both swung rights, then lefts, and all four connected. The sounds were like a boat oar hitting a bull's flank, solid and smashing and enough to kill a man like me. Neither of them staggered; they just moved around and shook their hands and got ready for the really tough work. This was so much warmup to them.

When they did start, the power and surge of the fight pushed my heart into my throat. They stood toe-to-toe and battered at each other, and I watched the small cuts jump out on their faces and the blood fly and speckle their bodies and stain their fists. Mixon broke through the first time and ran Dan backwards, smashing hammer blows to his body, then shifting to the head, then getting Dan half-turned and slashing a vicious rabbit punch behind his ear; it landed high as Dan ducked down and in. And then, as quickly, they reversed. Dan caught him by the neck and the pants and swung him in the air; it was impossible but Dan did it. He swung him and whirled him and threw him to the ground. I felt it shake under my feet and thought this fight was finished.

Dan stood five feet away, watching him. Mixon hit solidly, bounced, rolled over, and came to one knee. He grinned crookedly and spat blood and said, "A nice one, bucko," and was up and rushing before I got my breath.

They fought all over the yard. Mixon rushed Dan toward the water trough, got him backed against it, and caught him high on the head with a looping right. Dan went over the water trough, all the way, and lit on his feet. He shook his head and grinned, and came around the trough. Then Mixon started his tricks, and then Dan gave me the surprise of the fight.

I remembered him telling something about old Sam knowing a few Indian fighting tricks; and when Mixon moved in to try his arm-breaking and groin kicks and the like, Dan met him with as much and more. Mixon missed a kick to the groin and Dan raked him across the eyes with his thumbnails so the blood blinded Mixon for a moment. Dan ran backward six steps while Mixon was backing himself, covering up and wiping his eyes clear; and then Dan came forward on the dead run and threw his body into Mixon. Mixon went down with Dan's shoulder grinding into his stomach, slid, turned, and wiggled loose. Dan was up, catlike, waiting for him.

Dan said, "Had enough dirty stuff, Mixon?"

Mixon grunted and shook his head. He knew when he'd met his match. He dropped back into fighting stance and rushed. Dan brushed aside his arms and clubbed him on the cheek. Mixon spun around twice from the blow, his arms swinging loose like those on a little girl's rag doll, and fell to his knees. Dan dived for him and they rolled over together.

I couldn't see too much through the rising dust, but nobody was out, that was a cinch, because I could hear them grunt and gasp, and their elbows came up like pump handles and smashed downward into the dust. Then they rolled over in the grass under the trees, and Mixon tried to gouge

Dan's eyes, and Dan exerted some hidden burst of savage strength and flipped backward and completely over on his feet. Mixon's fingers were sticking straight out and stiff, where Dan's eyes should have been. Dan leaped forward and I heard the snap, and Mixon was swaying on his feet and holding his left hand. Dan had broken three fingers as easily as I would snap a twig.

Dan said, "Got enough?"

"Hell," Mixon said thickly. "Come on!"

He crooked that left arm so the elbow stuck up at Dan, and fought behind the elbow. He kept smashing in, and Dan took one and dodged two, and started to work on Mixon's stomach and sides. Mixon turned sideways and ducked into the blows, and Dan clubbed down Mixon's left elbow, got in a smash across those broken fingers that made Mixon cry out horribly, and then seemed to lose his right fist in Mixon's side.

I am sure that was the deciding punch. They fought another five minutes but Mixon was visibly hurt after he took that punch to his kidney. He fought until he was out on his feet, always boring in, and Dan cut him to pieces and straightened him out, and hit him on the jaw so hard that Mixon was off the ground with all of his body for a long moment, and then crumpled on the grass. His mouth was lax and wide open, and he snored, and he was covered with blood and dirt.

Dan looked down at him and turned to me. "I think he's out, Jim."

"You all right?" I asked.

Dan grinned through his own dirt and blood and said, "Take care of him," and walked to the river. I heard him washing all over, swimming and ducking under, and coming back to the gravel bar.

I got a pail of water from the trough and bent over Mixon. I wet my handkerchief and spread it over his face, and cupped small handfuls of water on the handkerchief and said, "How do you feel?"

"Water?" he asked thickly.

I canted the bucket and he gulped a third of it down, cleaned out his throat and mouth, and lifted himself on one elbow. He said, "Pour it on my head."

I poured it all on his head, got another bucketful and did the same thing. He got to his knees and shook his head and looked at me. His face was nearly unrecognizable. He spoke with difficulty as his mouth began to swell. He said, "He took me?"

"Yes," I said. "But he'll never have a tougher fight, against a better man."

"By God," he said. "That's the first time I've been laid out by a fist."

He winced and looked at his fingers and felt his left side with his good right hand. I said, "Can you ride to town? You better see Doc."

"I can ride," he said.

I helped him across the yard and got his shirt and hat while he pulled on his boots with his good hand. He couldn't straighten up and his one open eye glared at me redly through the red, bloody mask of his face. "Five days, Stanton. Then we start the ball. And tell Hannigan I rank him next to you."

"You're still alive," I said. "Go home and count your own beads. I'll give you five days."

He turned and walked crookedly to his horse, and I noticed for the first time the definite and peculiar pattern his boots made in the dust, the wide smooth wedge of the sole dented in a series of deep gouges made by some kind of huge round-headed cleats. A nice weapon in a fight if he had to use those boots, I thought, a nice clean way to kick another man's brains out while he lay in the dust. I watched him struggle into the saddle and give me a last look and ride for town.

Dan came from the river, buttoning his shirt and wiping his washed, wet face with the tail. I looked at him and said, "I'll be damned."

His body would have bruises, plenty of them, and his face was cut and bruised badly enough but without a single bad, lasting mark. His teeth were intact and he'd saved his crooked nose this time. He said, "I've been needing that one for a year, Jim."

"Where did you learn to fight?" I asked.

"Fighting," he grinned. "How do you think I got this nose busted the first time?"

"Club, maybe," I said. "Not fighting."

"You're right," Dan laughed. "I learned partly by fights, Jim, but a lot more from Sam and Doc."

"Doc!" I said.

"Sure," Dan said. "He can't fight but he knows all the tricks and he showed me how to do them. I coulda busted Mixon's arms and legs, one at a time, if I wanted to be real mean and nasty. Sam knows one where you break an arm. . . ."

"Never mind," I said. "You'll pass muster. But he's after you now. Told me to warn you. Before you came, he tried to dicker, just like Bisonette, and then gave me a week to clear out. After that"—I tapped my gun butts—"no more playing around."

"Fine," Dan said. "Now that we got everybody mad at us, I'm going down and have Mary patch me up. You come for dinner."

"Without warning her?" I said. "You can't do that to a woman, Dan."

"You don't know Mary," Dan said proudly. "You be there by noon or we'll come and get you."

I said, "All right, Dan, but it's your idea. And you tell

her so. You're the prospective bridegroom and you'll take the punishment.''

"Sure," he said, and his eyes looked wistful. "When I get enough money, Jim, we'll head for a preacher so fast we'll start a grass fire on the way."

Then I thought I knew why Mary was saving her money, not telling Dan how much she had, which was a tidy little sum or I didn't know a careful, saving woman when I saw one. I thought of all the money I'd won and lost, and played with like so much water. I said, "Don't worry, Dan. You'll make it."

I watched him go up the road and I thought, I could make a fortune with him and his fists, and he'd have his wife and his home. Then I shook my head, remembering the fighters I'd seen in the cities, beaten and off in the head. I went inside and coughed myself to bed. I remembered how Charlotte Bisonette looked in her red scarf, and that boy riding his pony beside the train coming into Weeping Water, and I saw Mary's calm face and murmured, "Dan, you lucky boy," and fell asleep.

Four

THE REST OF THAT WEEK PASSED WITHOUT TROUBLE.
September was melting into October and the leaves were
beginning to tinge and curl, and of all the seasons in this
valley, I was certain fall was the best. I spent most of the
time leaning against the grandfather of all cottonwoods beside the river where I had a clear view of the east bank and
all the valley sweeping beyond; and I slept twelve hours
each night and drank the milk Dan brought me each morning in a tin bucket, and thought about this business at least
fifty times each day. I decided that Mixon was either a
man of his word or so shoved up he didn't have the gump-
tion to make another try until his face and body and fingers
healed.

Dan and I were standing under the big cottonwood when
Doc rode out to see me on Friday. We sat under the cottonwood and watched the blackbirds chase each other in
the plum thicket across the river, and Doc told me that
Mixon looked as if he'd been shoved through a meat
grinder. Doc had spent two hours setting and splinting his
broken fingers and then ascertaining whether Dan's kidney
punch had torn him apart inside or just bruised him so bad
he couldn't touch himself without screaming. Mixon was

sticking close to his house in town and the farmers dropped by to see him and went away talking about men and what decent, God-fearing people ought to do about a no-good gambler spoiling the sanctity of their valley. That was clever of Mixon, I thought, stirring up the righteous people in his own behalf.

"How do they know who's good or bad?" I asked. "Or big or small, Doc?"

"Yes," Dan said. "How can you tell?"

"Depends on your point of view," Doc said, "And where you look from. See that mouse?"

The grass at our feet was long and thick, and a field mouse had built his nest under the waving, bending blades and was now, with no fear of us, running in and out of his nest, busy with some secret task and taking a second now and then to stare at us with his tiny, bright eyes, and then scamper away, tail wiggling.

"That mouse is small," Doc said. "Like a lot of people. They run through tall grass in their own narrow little world and they never bother about standing up straight and taking a look at the rest of the world around them. They don't care, I guess, or else they don't want to know. And when a bolder mouse who's been down to the river and up to the road, and knows everything about the world, sneaks in among them and tells them that black is white and gold is green, why, they listen sagely and mumble back and forth, and that's that."

I said, "And you get enough mice believing in that bold, wise mouse and they'll try a lot of things they wouldn't dream of doing otherwise. Like a full ear of ripe corn in that field across the river. They like corn but they have to follow the farmer when he picks it and be content with a few kernels. Maybe they know the corn belongs to the farmer but he doesn't care if they eat what he drops. But this wise mouse can get them together, and they might swim the river and build a raft and bring home the whole ear that doesn't belong to them. And they wouldn't call it stealing because the wise mouse told them it wasn't."

"Ah," Doc said. "You're a funny gambler."

"For a doctor," I said, "you look like a fellow I knew in St. Louis. He was the best shell-game and three-card-monte man I ever knew."

Doc smiled faintly and said, "You know I don't have a license to practice in this state."

"Doc," Dan said. "Don't scare Jim. He might not trust you."

"Who cares?" I said. "Sometimes a man wonders why he has to have a sheet of paper when his hands and eyes and mind can prove their value without it."

"Jim," he said softly. "A man gets weary of routine, and the same faces, and stupidity in the things we should try to improve, and don't."

Then I understood almost enough; and I knew we were going to be friends. Doc was running from the past and forever hoping the future would bring him the tolerance and the free chance to do the things he believed were right. I knew he'd tell me more if I stayed in the valley a reasonable time, but that was something I could not foresee. But we talked freely then.

Dan watched us and listened intently. He was hearing about the worlds he did not know, and in seeing them through our words, gaining a deeper understanding of us.

I told them about my father who came from Pennsylvania and went down the river to New Orleans and married a girl there. I never saw that girl, my mother, she died in my first month of life. My father was a gambler and my early years were spent with an assortment of nurses and maids who washed and fed me, and stayed with me until my father came home from a boat trip or an all-night game. After my childhood, I went with him on the boats from

New Orleans to St. Louis and back again, so many times I lost count. I could tell more stories about New Orleans than was good for me. I was an oldtimer in McGrath and Company at No. 4 Carondolet Street and I said hello to Price McGrath and James Sherwood and Henry Perritt as one man to another when we met on the street or in their club. And I went with my father to the house of Curtius at Toulouse and Chartres Streets, where no one could play without character references and a formal introduction. My father played boston, chess and poker, but he was not too fond of this place because the limit was a hundred dollars a hand. I had no regular schooling but my father taught me a great deal more than I could learn from books and dried-up teachers who sat fuzzily in their robes and dealt out knowledge with a palsied hand. In my sixteenth year I sat in the games with him; by the time I was eighteen he admitted I was his master, not only with cards but with the guns he taught me to use. He was killed the next year on the *Nancy Lee*, shot in the back by a drunken planter from Georgia who couldn't play poker and blamed his losses on my father by cheating. He would not accept a challenge or draw at the table, but left the saloon and sneaked around to the forward door and shot my father in the back. It took me six months to find him, for I had stayed in New Orleans that trip. I caught him in Savannah, called him out, and shot him between the eyes. The next day Sumter fell and I rode north to join Hampton's Legion. Four years later I rode west. Since then I had done the only thing I knew well; I gambled and traveled and here I was.

When I finished, Doc said, "How old are you, Jim?"

"Thirty-two," I said.

"I envy you," Doc said moodily. "You have more time than I."

"Tell Jim about yourself," Dan said. "Go on, Doc. I want to hear it again."

"I've told you a dozen times," Doc said. "Can't you remember?"

"Sure," Dan said. "But I like to hear it every time I can."

"All right," Doc said, "Jim, I'll bore you, but sometimes it's best to know."

And then he told me about his own life. He was born and educated in New York, but traveled to Ohio to practice medicine because, as he said, a man had more to work with there, and he was not content or pleased with the methods of his colleagues. He spent four years in the war with an Ohio regiment and came home filled with the things he had learned the hard way—by having to do things he had never tried in private practice. Something happened to one of his patients—he did not elaborate other than explaining that the operation had been successful about half the time during the war, and was justified by the fact that without an attempt every patient died. So this patient died and public opinion rose. He sold his practice, his home, and saddled his horse. He traveled to California around the Horn, made a trip to Mexico, came up the river, found this place, and put down his roots. He did not have a license but people forgot about such a small matter when they lived fifty miles from the nearest legal doctor and needed help in a hurry; and when they discovered Doc could treat them and keep them alive, they simply ignored any question of a license and brought him all their aches and pains. Doc was fifty years old and still discontented and restless; he lived to look over the next hill.

We discussed my lungs and I told them I thought it was the result of night hours and too little sleep and too much drinking and smoking. Doc didn't agree. He pointed out the great number of similar cases along the gulf and the Mexican border, and it was his opinion the disease was passed on by people who caught it from other people. He did agree with me on my reasons in a way, but explained that he thought they had nothing to do with the disease but were merely factors which weakened my body and made it possible for the disease to enter and grow.

I enjoyed that talk with Doc and Dan more than I cared to admit; and I hated to see Doc mount his fat mare and trot back, as he put it, to mix sodas for the kids and give the ladies sugar pills for ailments they imagined.

Dan was fully recovered the day after the fight, and seemingly had nothing to do on his own farm after his morning's chores. He brought me milk and eggs to help out my diet of store food. Mary visited me late on Saturday afternoon, bringing two loaves of fresh bread and a pitcher of lemonade. We sat on the steps and watched the sun drop and talked about Dan and the things we both knew were just ahead. I don't know whether she felt the same way, but I promised myself silently to see her as few times as possible, and those with Dan around. I was a sick man, true, but not that sick. She was the kind of woman you barely noticed on first glance, and then she grew in your eyes every time you saw her. And she was Dan's girl, and that was as far as I let my thoughts wander.

When she started home, she said, "Jim, be careful at Bisonette's."

"I will," I said. "But don't worry. It's just a social call."

She frowned. "Bisonette is a smart man, Jim. And his daughter"—she hesitated, and I saw the look in her eyes—"his daughter is a wild, undisciplined young fool who makes eyes at every man from her father's foreman to Dan."

"So," I said. "At Dan?"

"Dan doesn't know it," she said. "Don't tell him, Jim."

"I won't," I said. "I'll see both of you when I get back Monday morning. We'll have another pow-wow."

She smiled and said, "I'm glad you came along, Jim."
Then she left me, holding the bread and lemonade. I went
back to the kitchen and ate half a loaf and drank five glasses
of lemonade, and wondered if Charlotte Bisonette were
really that way, or was Mary just a little jealous of her
money and clothes—all the things Mary didn't have. But
Mary's clothes were actually of finer quality than Charlotte
Bisonette's, old and worn as they were, and I had a sneaking hunch she owned some fancy dresses and other things
she was afraid to wear for fear Dan might get the wrong
idea. As for money, Mary would never be broke. She
wasn't that kind. She wouldn't be jealous; it wasn't her
way. So it must be true about Charlotte Bisonette.

Dan led the roan over Sunday noon and told me how to
get to Bisonette's ranch. It was twenty miles west of the
store and I was to follow the trail until I came to a small
creek running through a canyon, cross this creek, and take
the side trail up the canyon. The side trail lifted out of the
canyon and ran through big hills and I would come around
the biggest one and see the ranch. Dan wasn't happy about
me sticking my head in the lion's mouth, but I gave him a
job to do and he quieted down. I had gone over the store
stock and stocked up enough canned goods and dry food
to last me through the winter, and I told him to pack up
everything eatable left on the shelves that Sam could use
and take it down to Sam while I was visiting Bisonette.
The way I figured it, I wasn't running a store anyway,
didn't have enough money to stock it decently, so why let
the stuff gather dust when Sam could use it.

Dan said, "That's a smart move, Jim. They might try
to burn the store and you'd lose everything. I'll tell Sam
you want him to have it. He's mighty touchy about taking
anything, but I'll explain it to him."

"Do that," I said. "I'll see you no later than Monday noon. If I'm not back then, come for me."

He nodded soberly. "That I will. Good trip, Jim."

Dan rode on to see Mary and I pointed the roan for the west hills. It was early to start for Sunday dinner but I wanted to take my time and see the country and arrive before dark. I was reasonably sure nobody would take a potshot at me but there was no sense in stretching my luck too far. I waved at Dan and urged the roan up the west trail. We were over the first hill in ten minutes and riding into unknown country that lifted from farming ground to range land, some of the best I ever saw. The trail was well traveled and I let the roan pick his own way, while I tried to find something in or on this land that made Bisonette so anxious to buy a bulwark between it and the progress of civilization. I saw nothing but rolling hills and long grass and plenty of cattle grazing nose down.

When I came to the creek and turned north on the side trail, I reined the roan under a grove of cottonwoods and gave him a good blow, then a short drink, and tied him while I had my drink and washed my face and hands in the cold water. I wanted a cigar badly but chewed on a blade of grass and sat under the cottonwoods and watched the clouds chase across the sky. An hour later I rode up the canyon, it was about right to come a-calling on Sunday afternoon. All I needed was a handful of prairie flowers for the ranch belle.

I followed this trail up the shallowing canyon and was suddenly on rolling land, deep-grassed pastures nudging in against fat round-topped hills, with the Big Muddy bluffs clearer now to the north, and the horizon, seen between the hilltops, a smoky silhouette of blue and purple to the west. I came around a big hill, halfway up its curving flank, and saw the ranch buildings; and I knew then that Bisonette was more than his outward appearance told me.

The man had to appreciate beauty and love comfort to have picked and built such a home.

It lay across the valley between hills, on a flat piece of grassy land, with the barns and outbuildings grouped to the south and the house standing long and low in the center of a low-walled lawn. The outbuildings were painted white, the house was white with green shutters and a cedar shingle roof that contrasted softly against the green and white, and the surrounding hills that would turn brown soon. I saw men moving around the barns and a crew loading hay from one of a dozen huge stacks south of the yard. When I rode down the trail and came between the buildings, I saw the late flowers blooming in the yard behind that low wall, and smelled the hay and grain and the clean, sweet odor of clover drying in the mows. A big man—it was Clancy—came from the bunkhouse and watched me while I swung down and looked around.

"Go up to the house," he said. "Folks are expecting you."

He was looking at my coat and I glanced at his holster and gun. He flushed slightly and took my horse to the barn without a word. I went through a white picket gate, up the walk to the wide, deep veranda, and Charlotte Bisonette came from its shadow to greet me. For a brief moment, with the foolish thought of dead youth, I remembered a great white house in Richmond and a dark-haired girl in a hooped gown smiling at me from the steps. Then I shook her hand and held my hat in hand and said, "I hope I'm not late, Miss Bisonette."

"Just right," she said. "Come in, Mr. Stanton."

Here was another side of the coquette, the demure smile and perfect manners of the lady of a great house. I followed her down a cool hallway into their living room which seemed to cover the entire lower half of the house. Bisonette stood at the far end, hands thrust deep in his trousers' pockets, smoking a black cigar and trying to find a smile. Charlotte said, "Father, here is Mr. Stanton," and bent her head and disappeared into the depths of the house. Bisonette and I were alone in the big room.

"Sit down, Stanton," he said. "Drink—cigar?"

"Last week, yes," I said. "Not now, Bisonette."

He nodded shrewdly. "Doc been poking you?"

"His orders," I said. "I was run-down."

He motioned to a wide leather chair and I sat down and watched him sit deliberately across from me. He said, "I thought as much, first time I saw you. You listen to Doc, Stanton. He'll fix you up."

"Maybe," I said. "It's not important."

He leaned over a low table and poured himself a small drink of wine. He said, "Well, you've kicked the bucket in the well, Stanton."

I was certain he'd heard about Mixon and Dan. I said, "It was worth the result. You missed the best fight I ever saw."

He was interested despite the personal differences involved. He said, "Did Hannigan really lick him?"

"Go to town," I said. "Take a look—if Mixon shows his face within two weeks. It'll take him that long to eat through his mouth."

"That good," he said. "I always figured Hannigan was more than bone and muscle. A shame he won't talk business with me."

Now I was interested; this was something Dan hadn't mentioned. I said. "What did you offer him?"

"Why," he said simply, "ten thousand for his farm and a job with me if he wants it. A chance to start a ranch out here, if he cottoned to the business."

"That was a good offer," I said. Now we were talking as he wanted us to, moving back to my store without being sharp and nasty about it. I said, "And he said no."

"As you are aware," he said dryly. "You'll have to admit, Stanton, I've been the victim of the damnedest luck a man ever had. That fool Simpson literally giving you the property, Mary Carr influencing Hannigan, you being stubborn . . ."

"Cautious," I said gently.

"All right," he said. "Cautious, then."

He downed his wine and wiped his mouth and scratched his jaw. He said, "Have you thought it over, Stanton?"

Charlotte stopped us here, which was a good thing. She called, "Dinner is ready, gentlemen."

Bisonette got up and changed the talk, saying, "We'll eat first, then talk," and walked across the hall into their dining room. I followed him and Charlotte murmured, "Your arm, Mr. Stanton," and placed her hand on my forearm and steered me gently after her father. She wore a light, fresh perfume and had no resemblance to the bold-eyed tomboy who spied on me from the river bank.

We sat at a long walnut table, the three of us, Bisonette and I across from each other the short way, and Charlotte sitting at the head and playing the gracious hostess. We were served by a Mexican woman and her husband, and I knew Bisonette had not divorced himself completely from his old life along the border. I opened my napkin and wondered what to expect in the wilds. I was again surprised.

We had Spanish olives and a light salad with small sliced onions and a dash of garlic and herbs for a starter; then a heavy puree with croutons. The next dish almost fooled me when the old man served my plate. Who thought of *calamares con tinta* in the middle of nowhere? They were imported squids and when they are cooked the right way, you never forget them. And these were wonderful. I looked at Charlotte and smiled faintly. She sipped her water and laughed with her eyes. After that I had my choice of prime steaks broiled in their own juice, wild stuffed turkey, small roast pig, and finally a Catalan *olla podrida,* or to put it frankly in Spanish, a rotten pot. It's made from everything—pork, ham, pastas, potatoes, onions—whatever the individual cook thinks proper. I settled for one plate of it, remembering other times in Ybor City and Vera Cruz, and this was every bit as good. We finished with Cuban pancakes rolled in sugar, ice cream, red wine, and coffee.

I ate a small dish of ice cream and took my coffee black. Bisonette had eaten the kind of meal I used to get ten years ago. He lit another of those Cuban cigars, pushed his plate back, belched softly, and blew smoke at me.

"What's the matter?" he said. "Did you think we were savages?"

"Sir," I said gently, "Miss Bisonette, you are the cleverest father and daughter I have ever met. You give a man such a meal in a country like this, and he finds himself weakening." They looked at me quickly, and I said, "But only during the meal, being a heartless man. Now tell me—where did you get your cook?"

"Carlos?" Charlotte said. "We brought him with Maria and Jose. He is a . . ."

"Catalan," I said. "I know. It's wonderful to find such cooking in this country. I can understand why you brought him along, Bisonette."

"He is my friend," Bisonette said quietly. "Mrs. Bisonette taught him how to cook."

Then I knew where she got the black hair and the bright eyes. I wondered how long this girl had been without a mother. Hard to tell, I thought, watching them. They were proud people who did not show their emotions to strangers.

"Mr. Stanton," Charlotte said. "If you will excuse me, I'll join you later. Father, I'll tell Clancy about the hay. You stay with Mr. Stanton."

We rose and watched her leave the room, and Bisonette said, "Let's go over and stretch out," and I followed him to the living room. There, in the same big chairs, he patted his stomach a moment and smoked his cigar slowly.

"Now," he said, all business. "Forget the dinner. You're too smart to fall for that anyway." For the first time, I saw a twinkle in his eyes. "I gave you a week to leave the country, didn't I?"

I said, "You did. Two days left."

"Don't misunderstand this dinner," he said. "That was Charlotte's idea mostly. She hates trouble. So do I. I've seen too much of it. So have you. We're sitting on a hot pot right now, but if you think I won't back my word, think again."

I said, "I didn't doubt you, Bisonette. I know a man when I see one."

"Thank you," he said. "Just as I knew I couldn't bluff you after I acted like a fool and bid crazy on your land. But you can't win, Stanton. I said a week. That still goes. Two days from now if you don't listen to reason, you'll leave this country, standing up or lying down. I've got twenty men on this ranch. I can get fifty more in three hours. And you've got Hannigan and yourself. No one else will side with you. Don't expect them.

"I will tell you once more," he said carefully, controlling his rising anger. "Maybe I haven't made myself clear. I came up the trail from Texas ten years ago, Stanton. I'm a man who likes his space and his privacy. I liked what I saw as I rode north. I held my herd at the shipping point and covered a lot of ground. I found this country. I was the first man here. I went back to Texas and sold my interests and brought everything I kept with me. Some of my men came. And my servants. I built this ranch and I own every foot of its grass, every hill and draw and ravine. The others followed me up the trail and we built our own little world out here." He waved his cigar to emphasize his points. "I don't mind progress—is that what you call this land rush?—because I realize it has to come. But not on my land. That's why I want a solid, unbroken front along the Spring River. I want a lot of distance between my home and their caterwauling and plowing and Saturday nights in town. I don't want my daughter close to the things that valley will see when the railroad comes through. And now will you stop riding me about some damned unknown reason for my wanting that land? I've told you why I want it. Now make me a price."

He was so good I almost believed him. I said, "Ten million dollars, Mr. Bisonette."

He sputtered and gulped. He said, "Don't talk like a fool, Stanton."

"And don't give me all that soft soap and honey," I said. "The offer still lies between us. Tell me your real reason and I'll talk business."

He couldn't say a word; just stared at me and started looking for a gun or a club. Charlotte came suddenly into the room and I got up and buttoned my coat. I said, "Miss Bisonette, will you have my horse brought around?"

"Please," she said. "It's a long ride. Stay tonight."

He looked up, red-faced, and snapped, "Get his horse, Charlotte!"

She murmured, "Yes, father," and left us.

I looked at him and said, "Listen to me, Bisonette. Between now and Tuesday at midnight you'd better do something. Make your will if you want her to get this place." He opened his mouth, and I said, "Not yet. I'll talk a minute. Listen to me. You can get fifty men but don't lead them. And you'd better keep about twenty-five of them around you because the minute you come for me, I'm coming for you. Sure, I'll have Mixon on one leg and you on the other, but I'll get you both if I have to dig a tunnel twenty miles underground into this room to do it. You're a big man and you've had your way all your life, but you'll learn something one of these days. I won't tell you what it is. Every man has to discover that for himself. So it's Tuesday night. Thank you for a wonderful dinner and your company. I won't wish you many more of them.''

I turned and left his house, and found Charlotte holding my horse at the gate. I took the reins and she touched my arm and said, "I'm sorry, Mr. Stanton, Really sorry."

"Thank your father," I said shortly. "And be careful from now on, Miss Bisonette. He wouldn't want you hurt by carelessness or accident."

I mounted and she looked up and said, "I suppose Hannigan is with you?"

"Couldn't keep him out," I said. "He'll hold his own."

She said, "If . . ." and shut her mouth and ran for the house.

I wheeled the roan and walked him past the barns, and no one stopped me or spoke. I went around the curve of the big hill and took a last look at Bisonette's little empire and then rode for the river.

I wasn't expecting trouble when I came to the canyon and rode down to the trail junction. I stopped the roan to give it a short drink in the little stream when I heard a stick pop. I acted without thinking, the only way a man can, throwing myself off the roan and drawing as I fell. Someone shot three times, fast, and I rolled on the gravel, getting my elbows under my chest, and saw the flash of his rifle on the east side of the canyon, high up. I shot twice, rolled to the right six paces, and shot four times, spreading my rounds in that area. The roan bolted down the trail and I heard a yell of pain from my friend on the wall. I lay on the cold gravel and waited.

Whoever he was, he was hit. I heard him swallow a groan and edge backwards up the slope. I wanted to go after him, but I didn't move. Night work is all right if you know how, but I wasn't Sam Ronson. He hit a jack pine and cursed, and then he made the top and I heard a horse snort and brace as he mounted. Then he rode east and north, and the canyon was silent.

I got up and walked slowly down the trail, wondering who was bossing this deal. Not Bisonette. He had honor. Mixon? I doubted it. But it had to be them or Higgens, and Higgens had been a Bisonette men. Or was he? I was cloudy on that man. I hadn't dug into his past deep enough. Maybe, if he was my bucko, it was a personal matter for kicking him out of the store. I didn't like it, not because I'd been shot at again, but for the reason that it complicated matters. Instead of two factions hating each other, and both after my scalp, I had a third man, maybe more, working on me.

I faced the prospect of a fifteen-mile walk to the store if Dan's roan decided to head for his home barn; and I couldn't make it and stay healthy. I got a lucky break with the roan. I found him at the trail junction, the reins caught in that big cottonwood's lower branches, where he'd swerved off in his fright. I talked to him gently and patted his neck and looked him over for a bullet crease. I found one across his mane, just breaking the skin, and understood his bolt. I led him across the creek and up the cut from the canyon before I mounted, and then rode him slowly all the way home.

Coming down the last hill, the river was a silver line curving between the dark banks under the small third of a harvest moon. I was getting spooky now, and dismounted before I reached the main road. I led the roan in a big circle that brought us into the trees behind the store, where I unsaddled him and slipped his bridle and turned him loose. He nuzzled me for a moment and then trotted for home. He'd go straight to the barn and Dan would find him in the morning; and that was how I wanted it, for Dan would come on the run.

I let myself in the kitchen door, blocked the window, and made coffee. Then I want to bed. It was just two A.M. Less than two days before the trumpets blew.

Dan's knock was like the morning we met. He shouted, "Jim, you in there?" and his voice showed his worry. I called, "Right with you, Dan," and let him through the kitchen door. He hadn't bothered about buttoning his shirt and pants, and he had one boot on and the other stuck in his belt. He started talking before he got inside, saying, "God, you gave me a scare, finding old Mose like that. Don't you ever scare a man like that again, Jim. How come you never stayed with Bisonette last night?"

"Sit down," I said. "I'll tell you."

I fixed breakfast and told him everything. He said, "Higgens, I'll bet. You think you nicked him?"

"More than a nick," I said. "Is Doc the only one in the valley?"

"Yes," Dan said. "Nearest one is Weeping Water."

"We'll go to town," I said. "I'd like to sit around and talk with Doc."

Dan said, "Oh, sure! Come to think of it, I got a lot to talk about myself."

"We'll not tell Mary," I said. "Not right now. She's got enough on her mind."

"She's awful worried," Dan said. "We talked last night and she told me something I think is a good idea."

"Yes?" I said. "Go on, talk. I'll get dressed."

"We're gonna have trouble in a little while," Dan said. "And maybe you and me might not be lucky. Mary said we could sell her our places for a dollar each, to make it legal, and get the deeds witnessed and registered and everything, and then Bisonette and Mixon would be no better off than before because they wouldn't hurt a woman.

She said maybe if we did that right now, and let it out, it might stop the trouble before it started."

I hadn't thought of that trick; it was a good one, too. But there was another side to it. I said, "Mary's thinking straight there, Dan, and I'm all for it, but remember this: if we deeded her our places now and told it around, that wouldn't stop them. They'd still try for us and use that as a club over her. See what I mean—they'd let her know if she didn't sell, you'd be shot. No, let's not rush anything. We'll play the string as far as we can, and if it looks like a showdown, then we'll do it."

"That's what I told her," Dan said. "I said you'd figure it the same way."

"Good thinking," I said. "Now let's visit Doc."

I began to think, at sundown, that I'd been dreaming someone shot at me and got nicked in return. We loafed in Doc's back room from morning till darkness and the only sick people we saw were two boys with stubbed toes and a sharp-nosed lady who wanted something to tone her up. Doc sold her a bottle of liver pills and, after she pattered out, told us, "The old jaybird needs a good shot of hundred proof." But no one with a gunshot wound staggered into the drugstore and fell on the floor. We tried to talk away the afternoon and growing weary of that, played a few hands of stud poker for matches. Doc asked me to explain about that three-card-monte and shell-game man I'd mentioned a few days ago; and I got three walnuts from the kitchen and a dried pea, and showed them how the shell game went, and with a deck of cards demonstrated the three-card-monte. I stood behind the table and rolled the pea around the three half walnut shells and imitated my friend, saying, "Gentlemen, pick out the shell the ball is under and you get five dollars," and capped the pea and shifted the shells. Dan grinned and poked one big finger at the right shell. I said, "The gentleman wins," and showed them the pea under that shell. Then I did it again and shifted the shells and when Doc pointed to a shell, I showed him all three shells—with no pea under any of them. Then I opened my hand, palm up, and showed them the pea held in my little finger. The three-card-monte worked on the same principle and I showed them how the dealer showed the sucker three cards—say an ace and deuce and three spot—turned them down, shifted them carelessly and asked him to pick out the ace. Of course, the sucker does. He knew because he noticed that the ace had a slightly turned up corner. I had Doc pick out the ace the next time and when he pointed and turned the deuce, I showed them how the dealer bent the deuce at the last second, smoothed the ace, and took the sucker neatly into camp.

Dan said, "I'll never play cards with you, Jim."

Doc just grinned and fixed supper, and I cleaned my guns and rested an hour on his leather couch in the big room behind his little office. This was his operating room and I couldn't help but notice how clean it was. And all this time we hadn't mentioned the shooting to Doc. When we finally told him, after supper, he smiled and shook a finger under our noses.

"I deduced something fishy," he chuckled. "Loafing here all day for no reason? Not you boys. Got any idea where you hit him, Jim?"

"No," I said. "It was dark and uphill, Doc."

"Don't be impatient," Doc said. "These boys won't come in until they're neck deep in a grave. But understand me—no trouble if we do have a visitor or I get a country call."

"No trouble," I promised. "Just a good look at him, Doc."

"Fair enough," Doc said. "Can't blame a man for entertaining his friends if you happen to be here."

110

"Maybe he didn't make it to town," Dan said. "You figured that, Jim?"

"He made it," I said. "He got his horse and cut the dust. He'd make it to town."

We talked about going on a hunting trip with Sam Ronson if we all lived until late fall; and just as Dan was saying, "You want to hit a deer right behind the shoulder," someone tapped on the back door.

We knew it wasn't a neighbor with a cup, to borrow some sugar. People don't tap that softly or come around in back unless they were afraid of something. We all did foolish, thoughtless things. Dan threw the cards at the couch and they fluttered all over the floor. I unbuttoned my coat and then shined one boot against the other. Doc jumped a little and wrote something in his nervous, scrawling hand on a scrap of paper, stuck the pencil in his mouth, spat it out, and went to the back door.

He opened it a crack and said, "Yes?"

Someone said, "Doc, lemme in, for God's sakes!"

"Who is it?" Doc snapped.

"Clem Roland," the man said. "I got Bill Higgens here—in bad shape, Doc."

Doc threw the door open and a skinny man I'd never seen before helped Higgens into the room. Higgens was covered with dried clay and bits of grass, and his right arm was wrapped in a dirty bandage that was soggy with blood around his elbow and caked dryly toward his hand. He'd been hit and made his run and tried to bandage and dress his own wound. I could visualize the result: dirt in the hole, wherever I'd shot him, and fever rising in his body and the wound getting sore and turning red. Higgens looked like death itself.

Doc said, "Over there—on the table. What happened?"

Roland said, "He got shot, Doc."

"When?" Doc snapped. "Who?"

"Last night," Roland said, helping Higgens onto the table. Higgens hadn't opened his eyes. Roland said, "He was potshot."

Dan grunted and looked at me. I shook my head for silence.

"Last night!" Doc exploded. "And you brought him in tonight, you fool! You ignorant, miserable fool. How long do you think a man can live? Get out of the light. Dan . . ."

Dan said, "Yes, Doc?"

"Light the bracket lamps," Doc ordered harshly. "Get those reflectors set. Jim, you heat some water, a lot of it."

Higgens opened his dust-caked eyes and tried to lift his head when Doc spoke. His mouth opened and he made hollow, vacant, hopeless sounds. Roland jumped and whirled and said, "Hey!" and stared wildly at the door.

"Potshot?" I said softly. "Roland, you pitch in here and help. Maybe we'll talk about potshots later."

Roland gulped and stammered, "Yes, sir," and ran for the buckets.

Higgens had given up hope when he saw us. He closed his eyes and I think he expected another shot between his eyes. He didn't move while we heated water and Dan lit the bracket lamps that were fastened to the walls in the corner overlooking the operating table. Doc laid out his instruments on a little white table he wheeled from the corner beside the table. He had changed abruptly from a pleasant little fat man to a quick-tongued, sure-fingered craftsman about to perform the job he knew best; and while he adjusted the reflectors to shine all light possible on the table, he removed the dirty bandage from Higgens' arm and examined the wound. And he talked a blue streak, to himself, in a sharp vitriolic monotone.

"Damned fools," he said. "Look at that elbow—wait a day—lost a gallon of blood—not to mention the alcohol—

have to come off—no other way—gangrene—may be drain-
ing inside already.''

I do not know a great deal about medicine, other than
simple precautions and field methods of dressing wounds,
but I learned a good deal that night, standing beside Doc
while he worked over Higgens.

I had shot Higgens, by luck, right through the middle of
his elbow. The slug had smashed on through and made a
tangled ruin of his arm. I had seen too many wounds like
that one in the war; the bones were splintered and the skin
was already drawn drumhead tight and blood was all over,
dried and caked and still seeping forth. Doc peered into
the armpit and said, ''No suppuration . . . Water boiling,
Jim?''

''Boiling,'' I said.

Doc poured half a bottle of some solution in the big pot
of boiling water, dropped all his instruments into the water,
and then washed his hands and forearms thoroughly in
nearly boiling water. Then he grabbed a flat screen and
held the instruments in the pot while we tilted it and poured
the water out. He placed the instruments on the little table
and, never slowing below a fast trot, got an odd-looking
mask and returned to the table.

''All right, Higgens,'' Doc said. ''Close your eyes and
breathe deeply.''

Higgens decided we weren't going to kill him after all,
and opened his eyes. He said weakly, ''You gonna cut it
off, Doc? Don't . . .''

''You want to live?'' Doc said.

Higgens whispered, ''Yes, Doc,'' and shuddered and
closed his eyes.

''You waited too long,'' Doc said. ''Last night we had
a chance.''

''I . . .'' Higgens said.

"Shut up," Doc said. "Dan, you know what to do. Remember that farmer you helped me with."

Dan went around to the head of the table and took the mask between his fingertips and placed it over Higgens' face. Doc opened another bottle and started the chloroform. Higgens shivered and rolled a little, and then began breathing gustily. Doc said, "Watch him close, Dan," and went to work.

Doc placed a tourniquet on the upper arm, twisted it and tied it. He took a scalpel and ran it over the arm, pursed his lips, muttered, "Steady, there now," and the scalpel cut cleanly and surely into the white bloodless flesh. Doc cut through and I saw the raw red muscle underneath. Doc said, "Higher now," and cut through to the bone. Black blood started to seep down and the scalpel touched the bone, and Doc cut all the way around the bone until I saw it, white and clean, deep in the mass of red flesh.

I wish I knew the correct way to describe the operation, for I know it was a wonderful job under the circumstances. But all I could do was wait for Doc's orders and watch him work. Doc grabbed a piece of linen from the little side table, wrapped it around the bone and somehow or other pulled the muscle and skin upward, so that about an inch or two of bone lay in the open. He said, "Jim, hold this! You wash your hands?"

I said, "Yes, Doc," and took the ends of the linen strip and held them against the pressure of the flesh, thinking then how I was responsible for this.

Dan said, "Oh, oh!" and gave Higgens more chloroform. Doc said, "Now," and took his saw and placed it on the bone. He said, "Roland, catch it when it falls."

Roland gulped and stammered, "Yessir," and stood by, shaking like he had the ague.

Doc started to saw and I bit my tongue for a moment then steadied and watched him go through that bone until the forearm and elbow shuddered humanly and came away in Roland's trembling hands. Doc was working faster than I realized as he took Higgens' pulse and muttered, "Damned fool," and snarled at Roland, "Well, throw it in the bucket," and went back to work.

I knew he was clamping the blood vessels but I couldn't follow all the movements of his flying fingers. He tied and tied, and then loosened the tourniquet and peered closely at the arm and said, "Ah, thought you'd fool me."

What he saw, he told me later, was the blood returning to small vessels he had missed and forcing them to bleed. He tied these and then did something he called ligating the cut ends, and folded the flaps of skin and flesh back, muttering, "No tension now," and working faster.

He placed a compress across the stump and bandaged it in place, and stepped back. He said, "Let him come out of it, Dan."

It was then I realized my face was wet with sweat. Dan lifted the cap off Higgens' face and corked the chloroform bottle. We moved around beside Doc and looked at Higgens. I thought he was dead but Doc grinned happily and said, "A nice job if I say so myself. If he wasn't strong as a mule, he'd be dead right now." He turned to Roland and said, "He'll have to stay here for some time. Can you watch tonight?"

Roland flicked his eyes at us, and then nodded. Doc went to a cabinet and returned with a hypodermic syringe and said, "He'll need a shot when he comes to."

We watched Higgens move slightly and open his eyes, blank then, and finally coming into focus. He stared at the ceiling and then looked around and saw Doc, Dan and, finally, me. And then he glanced down at the bandaged stump and started to cry. He had no courage or dignity, and he cried and then shivered and began to curse as the pain seeped into his body. Doc gave him the hypodermic and he looked at me and cried until it took effect and he dropped into deep sleep.

"Well," Doc said. "A welcome change from liver pills. Perhaps we shall have more business in the near future," and gave us a humorless smile.

"We'd better go home," I said. "Unless you need us, Doc?"

"I won't," he said. "You'd better get some sleep. I won't be responsible for Higgens when he wakes in the morning. If he saw you he might die from delayed shock."

I said, "A beautiful job, Doc."

Doc smiled wearily and said, "Compared to Vicksburg and a few other places, this was like loving a beautiful woman, Jim. But then, you should know."

"I know, Doc," I said. "It's still a beautiful job."

I paused beside the other table on my way to the side door and read the word Doc had scribbled when we heard the knock. It was "Higgens."

I said, "Good night, Doc," and followed Dan into the night.

The wind was cool and dry against my sweaty face, and it pressed my damp shirt against my back and chilled me.

Dan said, "Higgens is scared to death you'll go back and kill him with a soda bottle."

"Well," I said. "It was him. Now who's paying him, or was it his own idea?"

We walked rapidly through the quieting town, passing the saloons and seeing the slouched form of Marshal Brent just inside the Granger's Rest swinging doors; and moved swiftly down the road, our boots squishing softly in the dust. We swung into Mary's yard and she opened the front door and called, "Dan—Jim?"

"Sorry we're so late," Dan said: "We'll only stay a minute, Mary."

She said, "You were in town all day. What happened?"

Dan said. "You tell her, Jim."

So I told her everything and she stared at us and swallowed hard and leaned against the door. She said, "How terrible. Is he . . . ?"

"He'll live," I said. "But we can mark him off the slate."

"It's terrible," Mary said bitterly. "All you did was make him leave the store, Jim. He had no reason to carry such a little grudge so far. Now everyone will be watching us."

"Better that way," I murmured. "Don't worry, Mary."

"But I do," she said. "For Dan—and for you, Jim. Higgens has friends."

I said, "Don't worry, Mary. It'll make you old. It isn't worth the thought."

Dan said, "We better hit for home. Good night, Mary."

She said, "Good night, Dan—Jim."

"I'll be up about noon," Dan said, as we turned to the road. "That river fence of yours needs fixing."

Riding away, I remembered that she hadn't invited us in. But it was late and I couldn't blame her. When we said good night at the store, I smiled at him and said, "One day of grace left, Dan. I've got a few ideas for tomorrow night. We'll sleep on them and talk tomorrow."

Five

DAN REPAIRED MARY'S RIVER FENCE THE NEXT AFTER-
noon and came to the store at four o'clock. He wondered
about my rush for making plans and I tried to explain the
philosophy of men in the shoes of Bisonette and Mixon.
They had handed down a deadline and now they would
have to back their boast or lose face in the eyes of their
men and themselves. We knew Mixon was temporarily under the weather, so that left Bisonette to make the first
move. Not that it would be a serious effort to wipe us out;
it would be more of a feeling-out attempt to test our re-
sistance. I explained the principles of warfare to Dan: the
scouting, the patrols, assembling all available information
concerning the enemy, two or three fake sorties, and finally
the big all-out attack. Tonight would be a combination of
scouting and feeling-out. Therefore, I discussed this attack
and planned accordingly.

One thing I insisted on: we would not stay in the store.
That was the worst possible location for a defending force
of two, fighting as we were against twenty or more men.
We took a slow and careful walk all around and over my
quarter section which lay in a solid square with its east line
on the river, its north bordering Mary's place, and its south

against Dan's line. The west boundary was well across the main road with the ranchers' trail cutting through it to the junction with the main road. The land was flat and had never been cultivated, and the grass was long and thick, and the trees grew mostly along the river except for a small grove of beeches in the northwest corner across the main road. It did not offer much cover to an attacking force, and conversely, it had a like amount for the defenders unless they crouched behind the river bank. But I was expecting a night attack, and darkness is a cover-all for both sides.

"Where will they come?" Dan asked, when we finished our walk and returned to the store.

"I say right down the road," I said. "Riding fast and shooting, and maybe trying to fire the store. The logical direction is from town or down the west trail. I don't think they'll cross the river north and south and then try to force the ford. They'd be dead pigeons in the water. Now, we'll be outside. You tell me where the best two places for us are, close to the store, but not too near."

"Northeast and southwest," Dan said instantly. "One on the river bank, the other across the main road and south of the west trail in that little ravine running down to the river. I could squat there. You could be northeast of the store. That way we cover the roads and won't have blind spots they can duck into."

"Fine," I said. "And here's another possibility, Dan. They might scare us here and try to burn your place. We've got to consider that, although I think their own honor will make them try the store first."

"We're still all right," Dan said. "They can't get near my place without me hearing them. We'll take that chance. What time you want me up here?"

"We'll get settled right after dark," I said. "Plan on staying out all night. They'll make their play about midnight, but you never can tell. One of them might have Indian blood and like dawn better.''

''Want to get Sam?'' Dan asked.

''No,'' I said. ''I thought about that. We'll handle this one on our own. Sam will understand. Another thing—I'm not out to kill anybody—yet. Hold your fire until I open if you possibly can, and then shoot low. A few legs and some dead horses aren't as bad as dead men. You can get over a leg and buy another horse, but a dead man is the hole you can't fill. With another man, yes, but not in your heart.''

''That's white of you,'' Dan said quietly. ''Considering the way they've been potting at you. Anything else?''

''Nothing much,'' I said. ''Don't stick your head up foolishly. But you know that.''

''Sure,'' he grinned. ''I'll watch out for Dan. You keep both eyes on Jim.''

We fiddled around the store until late afternoon, sweeping the floor and swamping it out with a barrel of river water. We'd been talking earlier about a dawn Indian attack, and about the time I remembered my words, two reservation Indians came into the store and stood, leaning against each other, staring at me solemnly. I could smell the cheap liquor on them across the full width of the store, and I wondered who the brave, upstanding man was in town, selling them whisky, and taking their last cent. They were fermenting inside, and miserable outside. One of them looked at me and said, ''Pants?''

''Yes,'' I said. ''Pants.''

He spread his arms in a gesture of supreme futility. ''No money.''

I looked at those two ragged, forlorn men, made that way by the great wisdom and treaty-breaking lies of our politicians, and I thought, There stands Stanton, but for luck, and decided to give them a shock they'd never forget.

They turned to leave and I said, "Wait," and crossed the store and looked at the stacks of clothing Dan and I had been sorting out to keep for our own use in case the store did burn. I grabbed four pairs of pants, six blue shirts, two pairs of boots, two bright red bandanna handkerchiefs, and dropped everything in their arms. I said, "On the house," and when they shook their heads, I grinned and patted their shoulders and said, "From me, to you," and they got that.

The last I saw, they were running toward the river to change clothes and admire each other. For all I ever knew they took those new clothes to town and traded them for more whisky; but I didn't care. It made me feel good.

"You blamed fool," Dan said. "What'd you do that for?"

"We can't wear everything," I said. "They can. *Como no?*"

Como yes," Dan grinned. "Help me bundle these up."

We made a big pack of the clothes and boots and Dan rode home at sundown, leading the roan, to make anyone watching think I was settling down for the night. The roan jumped angrily under that insulting load of pants, shirts and boots. I put supper on the stove and tied a burlap sack around my waist to keep my pants clean; and that was how Mary found me five minutes later.

She opened the kitchen door and saw the burlap apron and laughed so hard she had to set her basket on the table and wipe her eyes. It was the first time she'd let herself go in my presence, and I was pleased to find a healthy appetite for laughter behind that calm, solemn face. She showed me the basket's contents: fresh bread, honey and a slice of red watermelon.

"You look wonderful," she said. "The perfect house-wife."

"With one decent pair of pants," I said, "a man has to use his head."

"Or a sack," she smiled, and then sobered. "I saw Higgens this afternoon, Jim. Doc let me peek in back."

"Alive?" I asked.

"Getting along fine," she said. "Doc told me a month would see him well."

"Too bad," I said evenly, and looking up, saw her eyes on my face, sad and something like a small girl seeing the school bully in his true light for the first time. I said, "Don't you want me to be honest, Mary?"

"Yes," she said slowly, "but it's a terrible thing, this shooting. I wish there was some way to settle everything without it."

"Your idea about deeding our place to you was fine," I said. "But Dan told you why I was against it for a while."

She nodded. "I think I understand, Jim. If I knew you better, then I'd know."

"No," I said. "You don't want to know me better, Mary. But I'll promise you this: if things look bad, we'll deed to you. They won't touch you."

"That shows good judgment, Jim," she said softly. "And I'll let you decide the time. It's bad enough now, sitting at home, wondering when . . ."

"The bread is light," I said quickly. "And the honey looks like canned sunbeams. I'm afraid I'd starve if you didn't think of my stomach."

Her eyes thanked me for stopping any outward sign of emotion. She said, "I'll have to run now, Jim. I'll be home tonight if—if you need me."

She stepped outside and we stood a moment, smiling at each other, and were that way when Charlotte Bisonette rode into the yard from town, sitting straight and handsome on a beautiful cream stallion. She pulled up beside us and smiled at me, and not at Mary.

I said, "Miss Bisonette."

She looked at Mary then, and said, "Good evening, Mr. Stanton—Miss Carr."

"You look lovely," Mary said sweetly. "On that beautiful horse."

I'd almost forgotten how women can pierce each other with their little, foolish words. Charlotte flushed and touched the big horse, and he jumped sideways, his long tail flicking very near Mary's shoulder. Charlotte controlled him with a soft word and a hand, and said even more sweetly, "Thank you, Miss Carr. But don't misjudge Pablo. He is beautiful but dangerous."

Mary turned to me and said, "I'll have to go, Jim. Good night."

I said, "Thank you again, Mary," and watched her move away through the trees on the river path leading from the store to her place. Charlotte let her get out of earshot and laughed at me.

"Helping Hannigan out?" she said. "Or yourself?"

"Don't let your temper run wild," I said. "Like your horse. It's the mark of a little girl with dirty knees and a bent for fighting in the dust."

She didn't answer me, and I rubbed one hand on the big horse's flank, feeling his smooth, long muscles, and said, "Do you think it's wise, Miss Bisonette, stopping here?"

"I was curious," she said. "I wondered if you had gone."

"I'm here," I said. "I'll be here tomorrow, and the next day, and the next, if that's what your father wants to know."

"I suppose Hannigan is following you like a cow on a rope?" she snapped.

"You may tell your father," I said, "that Hannigan will be here with me."

She wanted to say more, about what I could not guess,

123

but she turned the big horse and said only, "Watch yourself, Mr. Stanton," and galloped west. The last I saw was her straight back and flowing black hair against the skyline, and then she was gone.

I murmured, "Now why did she say that?" and decided there was no telling the ways of a woman.

Darkness was minutes away. I went outside and checked my guns and holsters, slipped an old brown sweater over my shirt, adjusted the holsters and stuffed extra rounds in the wide pockets of the old tweed coat, and found my supper burned beyond redemption. So I dined on fresh bread and golden honey, finished with watermelon and black coffee, and waited for Dan.

He tapped on the kitchen door after dark, and I said, "All right, Dan," and slipped outside, left the door unlocked, and followed him around on the river side of the store. He said, "I'll go down the river and come up the ravine. Let's go over everything again, Jim."

He wore heavy buckskins, the first time I'd seen him in hunting clothes, and carried his heavy rifle and a piece of plum club about three feet long, with a knobbed end big enough to smash an elephant's skull. He had a .44 stuck inside the coat, and the tip of a knife sheath poked from under the bottom fringe. He was ready for a small fight, a big fight, or a massacre. I felt good, just standing beside him.

"I'll shoot first," I said. "Then shoot low and keep moving. You know all that, Dan. If they make a try for the store, give them plenty of noise and they might break. After they pull out, wait fifteen minutes, and then come around to me."

"Got it," Dan said. "If I come around, I'll tap my stock three times before I climb the bank. Otherwise, shoot 'cause it won't be me."

I gave him a poke in the ribs and murmured, "Good

luck," and we separated. He floated down the path to the river and was gone in two eye-blinks, and I walked into the trees and turned north along the river until I reached the small hump of ground between two cottonwoods Dan had picked for me that afternoon.

I settled myself on my stomach between the trees, put my chin on the tower of my clenched fists, and stared at my store and the roads and the land beyond, flowing slowly toward the horizon. It would be a dark night despite the moon; clouds were running smoothly with a strong north wind that smelled of rain and rattled the leaves about my head. It was a fine night for sparking your best girl or killing your worst enemy. A stick made its presence known against my chest and I squirmed around and pushed it to one side, and hoped they would pay an early visit. I hated this waiting; it gave a man too much time to think and remember.

My father had once said, "Your memories are the sweetest part of your life but you'll never test them to the hilt until you are running out of life and then you take the time to dream and have them troop past your heart, so fine you can almost touch them."

I hadn't thought of those words in many years; and tonight they came back to me with the pain in my chest and the north wind helping them along, with my father's face behind them. I could see forgotten days again: the first time he took me to dinner at Antoine's and my deathless struggle with lobster and oysters on the half shell; that day on the river he taught me to fish from a small boat, wearing old clothes and proving himself every bit as wise in fishing lore as Big Joe, the boss stevedore on the *Nancy Lee;* the first girl I kissed, on Royal, late one night under an iron balcony; riding from New Orleans to Matamoros at the end of the war to see if there was truth in the story of a last-ditch Confederate Army marching to Mexico, still young enough to play the fool and go along; the feel of a new deck of cards; the mountains around Santa Fe at sunset, blood-red and white-capped; San Francisco after the war; taking a Yankee Clipper from San Francisco to Acapulco on a bet; the bay and the steaming dirty town with the mountains rising toward the sky; riding to Mexico City on a donkey; riding to Vera Cruz on a donkey; beating Malone to New Orleans to win our bet made in San Francisco, he going overland and me taking the Acapulco route; that woman on the train to Weeping Water and the diaper I changed; did that make me a better man; Doc's scalpel shining in the lamplight; a dead man on the saloon floor in Dodge City; Bisonette's cigars and his daughter's black hair; Mixon rolling with Dan on the dusty ground; Mary's cool, sweet voice; time running out.

Why get a bullet through my head for a principle, I thought. Or was it money? I didn't know, honestly, unless it all went back to the fact that a man has to live with himself; and sooner or later, no matter how bad he has been, he will have to make a stand to save his soul. I tried to weigh my own life against whatever the standards were, and I couldn't see where I was so bad or so good. Maybe it was a combination of bad lungs and bad luck, and hating to run from anything. But whatever it was, why ever I stayed on, I felt better about doing this than I had for a long time. And then I laughed softly and said, "No more thinking, Stanton," and rubbed my face and concentrated on the job ahead.

If I learned nothing more on that wait from first darkness to midnight, it was remembering once more how humpy and brick-hard the ground can be. I had forgotten the bivouacs during the war by this time, but my stomach and legs had better memories than my head that night; they were growling their protest at midnight. And then it happened.

I heard the horses coming from town and for a moment

126

gave them no thought. A bunch of boys going home after a few drinks and a game and some talk in town; and then I remembered that they hadn't passed this way going to town. I drew both guns and hugged the ground, watching the open yard around the store and the road junction gleaming dully under the cloud-filled sky. The hoofs drummed louder, broke from the trees along the main road, and then broke into a full run.

They came yelling and shooting into the yard and I heard the slugs rip into the store; and then they wheeled and dashed west and made a big circle on the meadow and headed back for another try. They didn't make sense; this was Saturday night stuff in Dodge City or Abilene, shooting up the town from an excess of sheer deviltry. They made this second pass and my windows shattered and fell out, and I heard a can inside, on the shelf, pop open when a slug blew it apart. I held my fire.

They ran down the road toward town and turned, and came past again, and this time the shooting was faster and their shouts louder; and I was beginning to call Bisonette, for this was his crew, a damned fool. Then I saw the flicker beside the store on the river side, down from me, and I knew Bisonette wasn't a fool. Or maybe it was Clancy, that tall, lanky foreman, ramrodding this deal. They had used good tactics. They raced up and down, shooting and yelling, while one of them sneaked along the river and came up to set the store afire. I saw that man push his burning, oil-soaked rags against the wall and run with the awkward movement of a man wearing boots, around the store and out to the road where they had a horse waiting. Then they pulled off a ways, up the west trail, and peppered the store with rifles and revolvers.

I pushed myself backwards and got behind the trees, and then ran along the river until I came abreast of the store. I took a quick look down the path, saw no one, and walked quietly through the last fringe of trees to the store wall. I kicked the burning rags away from the wall, got down on my knees and rubbed out the first embers, and turned to stamp the rags out. Someone shouted "Ho," from up the main road, and a bullet slapped into the wall above my head. They had men staked out to watch for this, and I was giving them a fair shot for their pains.

I bent down and ran for the river bank, and that man to the north let me hear from his country. He was shooting a repeater and he gave me eight shots in a row, each of them nibbling at my heels. I made the trees, jumped down the bank and landed on my feet, and headed upriver to give that smart bucko a taste of his own medicine. I ran fifty feet and scrambled up the bank, rested my elbows on the edge, and tried to locate the stakeout. He obliged me, shooting twice at the last place I'd been; and I gave him three, high enough to miss but close enough to scare. He yelled and the bunch of them whooped it up to the southwest, and Dan opened the ball with his rifle, firing so fast I thought he had a platoon strung out along that ravine.

Someone shouted, "They put it out!" and my friend along the main road yelled, "He's along the river," and threw a wild last shot at me, and took off, running through the grass for the main road. I gave him another high shot to speed him along, and made a quick run for my first position. Dan was firing from the ravine and they were slamming back at him, and I wondered if they were serious or just trying to scare us out. It was strange Bisonette hadn't used the hay wagon trick, lighting it and pushing it down the gentle slope, across the yard, and against the store front. I couldn't move a hay wagon, and he'd burn me out easy that way. Maybe, I thought, maybe he doesn't really want to burn the store. But that didn't make sense either.

Another voice—I think it was Clancy—shouted, "Come on," and they galloped west, stopped half a mile up the trail, fired a few token shots at the store, and drummed away over the ridge. And it was quiet again.

I waited fifteen minutes and then heard three soft taps on a gun stock. Dan came through the trees and dropped on his stomach beside me and said softly: "Nice night."

"Come close to you?" I asked.

"A mile away," he chuckled. "I saw that boy set those rags. You did a nice job, kicking them out."

"Bisonette?" I said.

"Not him," Dan said. "About fifteen of 'em. Sounded like a hundred the first time around. Clancy was there, and that young bronco-buster named Glidden. They sure acted like it was just fooling around, Jim."

"That's what it was," I said. "We'll stay here a while and then make a scout around."

We had no more trouble that night. I walked to town the next day and talked with Doc and looked in on Higgens, who gave me a sour stare and turned his face to the wall; and no one seemed to know anything about our trouble but the marshal. Brent was on the sidewalk when I came from Doc's drugstore. He saw me and said, "Heard you had some shooting out your way last night?"

"Boys going home," I said. "Trying to hit the moon. You ought to know that sound, Brent."

"Me?" he said. "How would I know?"

"Why," I said, "it's like the Texas brush poppers riding into Dodge City at night, Brent. Don't you remember?"

He stared at me thoughtfully, his long face creasing and scowling. He said, "I never been in Dodge City, Stanton. All I was gonna say was, if you had trouble, I've got no authority to help you out. You'll have to get the county sheriff from Weeping Water."

"Thank you," I said. "That's mighty considerate of you, Brent. If I did have any trouble, I think I could handle it myself."

"Think a lot of yourself, don't you?" he said.

I said, "Don't you?"

He didn't like talking; it takes half a mind at least to talk. He said, "Why, sure I do."

"Don't get lonesome," I said.

I don't think he got it until the next day. I walked down Main and out of town, and he stood in the same place before Doc's tapping one boot toe on the boardwalk and staring moodily across the street at the Big H. He didn't like me, and that made us even. I knew we'd have trouble if I stayed long enough, and I was just the fool who wouldn't mind trouble with a man like Brent.

Dan figured out the reason for our unexpected peaceful days and nights. After a week of quiet he told me it was because the farmers were busy with fall chores, corn picking and woodcutting and fence fixing, everything they had to do before winter stopped all work in the valley. Bisonette didn't have time to bother us, either, for he had a late fall gather to finish that took all his men. He couldn't leave his cattle out in the hills over winter as he had in the Southwest. He had to bring them in and hold them on the pastures and meadows, and feed them hay through the winter. And there was another reason I decided was just as important as the fall work.

Bisonette had made one try, mostly to scare me, and now was waiting to see if Mixon would act. And Mixon was barely getting up from Dan's beating, and no doubt waiting hopefully for Bisonette to try again. Everybody in town knew what was going on between us; and not a one of them but a little red-haired boy seemed to care. He paid me a visit the next Saturday, a sling-shot stuck in his hip pocket, and offered his services to me if I needed a good scout on weekends and after school. We had a nice talk and the result of that was, he came out after school three and four times a week, with two other boys who seemed to be his gang, and asked me a thousand questions about my guns and when I was gonna shoot the marshal and Mixon and Bisonette, and then make my getaway.

I thought his folks would hear about his visits and put a stop to them, but something happened during one of his visits that scared his two pals out for good, and only seemed to make him hang around closer than a burr on a burro's tail. It was late in the afternoon the following week.

Dan had come by on his way to see Mary, and I sat on the front steps and acted as judge while Red and his two buddies played Indian around the water trough and through the trees. Red had killed each of them fifty times, as befitted the brave scout, and they were getting a drink at the well and squabbling over who was going to be whom the next game, when a wagon came lumbering down the main road. It was old and travel-pitted, with equipment banging against the box, and the team was ready to drop of old age. A fat woman in a big sunbonnet was driving, and her husband, a skinny man in dusty pants and open shirt, was walking beside the horses. He saw the store and my trough, and turned his team into the yard.

"Got a drink, mister?" he said.

"Help yourself," I said. "All you want."

I wondered where they were from—Ohio, Illinois, Missouri. He didn't sound like a New Englander. He got his horses over the trough, and handed his wife a dipper of water. Red and his fallen Indians went over in the shade to wait until civilization passed on and returned them the field of honor. The woman finished her drink and he helped her to the ground, almost breaking the doubletree in two, and they came toward the store.

He said, "I'd appreciate a little shade, mister, if you don't mind. My wife's nigh to be getting the sun blindness."

The sun wasn't that bright, late in the fall, but I didn't

know if she had weak eyes. I saw Dan coming through the trees from Mary's, and I said, "Come in and rest," and led them into the store. I stepped behind the counter and turned, and saw him walking ahead of his wife. They got about halfway across the floor when he jumped to one side and his wife pulled a .44 from somewhere in that dress and gave me a steady, stomach-high look at the muzzle. He said, "Up, Stanton, up!"

His wife pushed the sunbonnet back and I saw the thickest set of black whiskers since Henry brought me into the valley on his freighter wagon. I said, "Yes?" and didn't move.

The man in the sunbonnet said gruffly, "Don't try it, Stanton. We ain't got nothing against you. Just lift 'em high while Jed gets your guns. Then we'll take a little ride."

Jed didn't have a gun on him. He came around the counter and I raised my arms. I saw Dan move through the door and swing his rifle, stock first. He clubbed the fat man in the sunbonnet so hard the .44 jumped three feet and was still dropping when Fatty dug his nose against the splinters. I said, "Welcome, friend," and hit Jed in the stomach and grabbed a can of beans and brought it up under his jaw. His teeth snapped like a castanet and I caught his shoulders as he collapsed, and threw him over the counter on the floor. Something whizzed past my ear and I looked up to see Red standing in the doorway, his slingshot vibrating from the force of his shot.

I said, "Red, you hit for home."

"You need help," Red squeaked. "I knew he wasn't no woman."

"Go on," I said. "And don't tell. And keep your pals shut up. Promise?"

"Can I come back tomorrow?" Red said eagerly. "Will you tell me where you buried them?"

"Sure," I said. "But we won't hurt them, Red. Now hurry up."

He ran for home and I looked at Dan and said, "Thanks."

Dan watched Red high-tailing up the road and said, "Little devil," and poked the fat man with his boot toe. He said, "Mixon?"

"Mixon," I said. "And a good try, Dan. A mighty good try. I don't know what their orders were, but I'd say to toss me in that wagon and take me to Weeping Water and put me in a freight car. Maybe."

"Yes." Dan said. "Maybe. We'll have a little talk when they wake up. By golly, I near broke my stock on that bonehead."

They wouldn't talk for quite a while, not until Dan told the fat man he'd just take him down the river, tie his arms and legs, and see if he could float to Weeping Water. The fat man couldn't swim. He gulped and said, "You wouldn't do that." and Dan said, "Got a rope, Jim?" and Fatty talked.

He didn't know who hired them. All he knew was, they were offered the job by a bartender in Weeping Water, and the bartender gave Fatty and Jed two hundred dollars and told them what to do. The bartender was gone the next morning. They got the wagon and Fatty dressed up, and they drove from Weeping Water to bring me back and deliver me, the next night, to someone in the railroad yards. That was all they knew. I believed them, all right. And I had a new respect for Mixon. We took their guns and Dan kicked them into the wagon, and they took off for Weeping Water a lot faster than they came up the road. We wouldn't see them again. They'd put a lot of space behind them before Mixon discovered they hadn't backed their play. And that was all the trouble we had until the first of November, unless I counted Red's attacks on the store after school.

The children seemed to enjoy fall weather more than their elders; perhaps it was because fall makes a man think of winter, and winter makes him count the years behind and the fewer years, always lessening, ahead of him, and that makes him sour. I watched the children moving over the valley in their small bands, like cavalry troops on reconnaissance or forage duty. They sneaked through a cornfield across and up the river from my place after school, and swiped watermelons and big yellow cow pumpkins from the fields; and they chased each other through the trees and up and down the river banks, and once they churned a path through a newly sowed field of winter wheat, and the farmer, who must have been grinning while they swiped his pumpkins and watermelons, came out in righteous wrath and sent them skedaddling for home. I watched them fish along the river, using corks they picked up behind the saloons for bobbers. They had a big bare yard behind the schoolhouse and I passed there a few times during recess and saw them playing one-o'cat and town ball and pullaway, and stink base and hide-and-seek. Once I saw a mighty good fight between Red and a bigger but more lethargic boy who seemed to think that size was all important. Red whacked him in the stomach and beat a tattoo on his nose and chased him into the schoolhouse. I decided that Red probably did a lot of things I knew nothing about, like throwing weeds and empty bottles on the drunks behind the saloons and spying on the young couples buggy riding along the river. I wondered about his parents, and watching Red and the other children, I felt my own childhood grow far away, as if it had never been and I was seeing the ways of a child for the first time.

When he came out the next day I said, "Red, you never told me your name?"

"You never asked," he said.

I grinned at him. "Now let me see. Chauncy, Algernon, Fauntleroy?"

"Them!" Red said. "I ain't no sissy. My name's Bill."

"Bill what?" I said.

He looked at me, and I saw the tears start deep in his eye corners. He said, "Higgens."

I didn't answer for a long time. What could I say? Finally I said, "You know how your father was shot, don't you, Red?"

He rubbed his bare toes in the dirt and nodded. "You shot him."

"You know why?" I asked.

"Sure," he said. "He drygulched you. He had it coming." He explained then, as fast as he could. "My mother, she don't live with him no more, Jim. She kicked him out a long time ago, when we first come here. We live behind Doc's, across the alley. Mother takes in washing and bakes bread for sale. She's a real good baker. I bring bread twice a week to Mary and other folks."

I said, "Mary buys bread from your mother?"

"Sure," he said proudly. "Twice a week."

I swallowed a laugh at the vanity of women. So Mary was buying that wonderful bread and undoubtedly practicing on the sly so Dan wouldn't think she was a greenhorn.

"It's good bread," I said. "I've had some, Red."

And then I couldn't stop him. He'd been wanting to tell me all about himself since the first day he came out. He wanted to tell me about Higgens drinking and getting into shady business, and how his mother washed clothes and baked bread and did anything she could to keep them, and how Higgens would sneak around at night, half drunk, and try to break into the house and Doc would come across the alley and send him away. He tried to explain why he had to lick all the kids in school. I didn't have to be told why; I knew why. And he finished by telling me how he wanted to help me lick Mixon and Bisonette because they had something to do, he didn't know for sure, with making his father as he was today.

I let him talk himself out, and then I said, "Red, I'd like to be your friend, if you'll be mine."

"Shake," he said.

He was an old man at ten, Red was, the way I hate to see a boy grow up. After he went home, I spent a bad night thinking about boys like Red and men like Higgens and what I could do about them. It seemed as if I spent the first three days of November thinking about Red. Then I had no time to think about boys.

Sam Ronson paid us an unexpected and hurried visit that third day of November. He stopped for Dan and they galloped into the store yard and ran into the kitchen before I had time to open the door. They waved aside my offer of coffee and started talking.

Dan said, "Sam's got some funny news."

"Funny," I said. "Like Mixon dropping dead or Bisonette falling off a cliff?"

Sam didn't smile and I knew he was worried. He said, "Mebbe it ain't much but it looks odd. I seen a couple of lads foolin' along the river these past three days."

Sam was mad. He didn't like strangers prowling on his private ground, which was how he considered the Devil's Cup. I said, "What kind of lads, Sam?"

"Engineers," Sam said. "Least, I think so. They got a couple pack horses, lot of crazy-lookin' possibles on their belts. I figures I better tell you."

"Engineers?" I said. "Or locators? In this country so late in the year? Who are they working for? Can we find out, Sam?"

"Why, sure," Sam chuckled. "I'm right anxious to palaver with 'em."

"Me, too," Dan said. "What are they lookin' for, Jim?"

"I don't know," I said. "Where are they now, Sam?"

"Five miles south on the east bank," Sam said. "Camped in a bed of cottonwoods. They build a fire big enough for fifty men each night."

"Well," I said. "They might be nothing, or they might be something. We'll pay them a visit."

"Tonight?" Sam asked eagerly.

"Think anybody'll bother us tonight?" I asked Dan.

"Folks are still busy," Dan said. "We got a few days left."

So we rode south that night and stopped across the river from their camp. We sat in a thick growth of willows while Sam went down for a closer look. He returned in ten minutes and said scornfully, "Settin' round their fire, writin' in black books and throwin' crazy language back and forth. You kin hear 'em a mile off. Come on."

I didn't question Sam. We crossed the river a mile down at a ford no one but Sam and Dan knew about, and came up the east bank and into the trees. Their fire was bright against the shadows and both of them stood up and watched us dismount and come forward. Dan was right. They were engineers on a job. I saw their instruments neatly lined up under a tree, their notebooks and packs and short carbine rifles leaning against another tree. They were young, about Dan's age, and pleasant-looking.

Sam said, "Howdy, boys. We saw your fire and stopped by."

The tall one said, "Won't you sit down? We're just putting on some coffee."

So we sat around the fire and they poured coffee and we told them we lived in the valley, and they talked about the hunting possibilities and the weather and finally Sam said, "What you doin' here so late in the year?"

The tall one grinned and shook his head. "Railroad work. The boss says 'go' and out we go. You know, of course, we'll be through here next year. The front office wanted a last checkup on flood signs and the general river data. They weren't too sure about the high water mark."

"And you're checking this far south of town?" I asked. I thought you were going to build through the town?"

Sam murmured, "River never goes over the bank down there."

They frowned and glanced quickly at each other, looking for mutual support. I began to smell something. It wasn't clear, but these engineers weren't nosing up and down the river for flood signs any more than we were.

I said, "The locators and surveyors and engineers have been riding through here for two years. Last we heard, your advance party was three hundred miles beyond here, well into the Green Hills."

"We know that," the taller one said. "But you know how the bosses are. They want everything checked a dozen times."

"No," I said. "I don't."

"If one look ain't plenty," Sam said, "man oughta be fired."

The tall one laughed and said, "I feel the same way, sir. I'd get more pay then."

They were beating around the bush with us. I took a blind shot up a dark alley, and said, "Well, the way it looks to me, maybe your company is getting ready to leave us sit high and dry, and go around the south bank of the Spring."

"Oh, no," the tall one said. "They wouldn't do that."

"They better not," I said. "We're not holding any land for a higher price, but we sure can use your railroad."

That seemed to strike their funny bones. They laughed and the tall one said, "I'm sorry, gentlemen, I really am, if you're worried about the railroad not coming through. I'm afraid we aren't promoting good feeling between our company and its future customers. But, honestly, our purpose is to check on floor stages and see how the water runs . . ."

"Time for that," Sam said dryly, "is spring o' the year. Come March."

No one spoke for a few moments. Dan moved restlessly beside me. I said, "You finishing up soon?"

"Today," the tall one said. "We're going to steal a day from the boss and do a little hunting in this wild country south of here. Then it's back to Weeping Water and the winter work."

"About that huntin'," Sam said gently. "No good south of here."

"No good?" the younger one said. "Why it's the finest . . ."

He stopped talking. Sam was looking at him across the fire. Sam said, "No good, son."

The tall one began to pull himself up. He said, "Now look here . . ."

It was time to play for the big pot; we'd prattled long enough. I said, "Sit down, friend!"

They jumped up and looked at two rifles and my guns. The younger one said, "Uh-uh," or something like that, and the tall one just swallowed nervously and stared at us. I said "Sit down!"

They sat down.

"Go over them, Dan," I said.

Sam and I watched while Dan searched them. Their only weapon other than the carbines leaning against the tree was a pocket knife in the tall one's right hip pocket.

I said, "I hate to do this, friend, but I'll have a look at your notes."

He was young and I guess he didn't know anything about the goings on above him. He wanted to chew up that notebook or kick it in the fire. I never saw such a faithful servant; the company would do well to watch him—if they ever knew.

I reached for his black notebook and began leafing and reading. Five minutes later, on a back page, I found the answer to everything we wanted. It was so simple, so easy. It was the same old story of big money and greed, and two men fighting for a piece of that big money.

These boys were looking for flood signs like I was looking for a gold mine. This was what they had been doing; and here, according to the time of each test, was something else. They had conducted all their work from Dan's place north of town, at night.

They had been checking the river banks and drilling core samples of the ground along those banks. Why? To find the best place to cross the river. And where were the best approaches for a bridge across the Blackwater in this valley? Where was this best location because of solid high banks clearing high water and making the wide swing along the west edge of the valley well out of flood range?

Why, right across the river onto my land. Right where the ford was, then west to the edge of the valley and north a few miles and then northwest toward the Green Hills along their already planned route through the land belonging to Bisonette and his rancher friends.

My worthless store and my quarter section of land! Dan's place south of me! Mary's on my north! And where would the town of Blackwater be when they changed the route? High and dry. And who would make a fortune because of the notes in this book, verifying that our land was the best place for high, dry ground for shops and sidings and all the buildings and equipment used in a division point on a railroad? Why, the lucky people who owned that land across the river.

I reread those notes, all his core sample tests, his conclusions: "ford south of town—store above ford—gravel and limestone rock—hard rock at ten feet—strata indefinite but sufficient—highest banks in valley."

I remembered Bisonette giving me that impassioned speech of his at his ranch. I remembered Mixon pleading because of all those eager, land-hungry settlers waiting for him to open the gates of heaven and me, the devil, holding them up.

Cattlemen against Grangers? Like hell!

I said, "Friends, we're sorry we had to get so tough. We don't want to hurt your principles, your morals, or your bodies. All we wanted was a straight answer."

"You've broken the law," the younger one cried. "You can't read our notes. . . ."

"Law?" Sam said softly. "Out here, son?"

He considered Sam's words for a moment, and shut his mouth.

I said, "Look, you know how we feel about your railroad, after reading those notes. Don't you realize your railroad is selling out a whole town? A town that was promised faithfully it would be on your main line? There's merchants in Blackwater who have sunk their last penny in new stores and stocks. People have built houses. And you two are low enough to come out here and change the route, and never give a thought to those people. By God, we ought to . . ."

"Now, wait," the tall one said. "It's not our fault, mister. We're paid to do a job and you know we've got to keep our mouths shut about company business if they tell us to."

"That won't cut it," I said. "You've got the souls of

two weasels. Why can't you recommend the crossing at the town? Would it be any skin off your nose?"

"Mister," the tall one said desperately, "give me a chance. This report of ours only verifies one made two years ago by other engineers. I don't know anything about it, but we hear a little gossip in the office and someone told me that a big man from St. Louis who owns over half the company stock had that first report made two years ago and it got lost and because nobody knew anything about it, we came on through and"—he spread his arms helplessly—"I'm no politician, mister. You know how it goes. Now that big man wants the route changed. Well, he doesn't have any actual position or any direct control over operations, but he owns the stock. Do you know what I mean?"

He was too frightened to lie—and it all added up. I said, "All right, friend. Here's your book. But just one more thing . . ."

They stared at me, waiting for a shot in the head, they were so scared. I said, "I see your names and home addresses in the book. Bob Olsen and Harry Henderson, Kansas City. Now I'll tell you something, friends. You go back to your office and forget all about this. Nobody looked in your book. Nobody knows anything about the route change. You turn in your report and go on about your business, and your lives. We won't tell anybody about this. But listen, friends. If that route is changed again, you won't be able to run far enough to get away because we'll hunt you down and we'll cut out your hearts and ram them down your throats. Understand?"

The tall one said, "Yes, sir. You can depend on us."

We got up and Dan brought our horses into the firelight. We mounted and I said, "Don't ever forget. Sleep and get up and head east."

Sam added softly: "No huntin'—remember?"

We rode north, all the way to the ford across from the

store, before it really dawned on Dan. Then I had to tell
him again. After that he kicked his horse and got us thoroughly soaked, running across the river. He leaped from
the saddle and did a flip in midair and came up yelling. I
didn't blame him.

I said, "Sam, how can I thank you for this?"

"Don't, Jim," he said. "Jest don't ferget where I live.
I got a hunch you'll be needin' help again."

"Yes," I said. "I know we will. And I'll call loud,
Sam."

"Man!" Dan said. "Wait till I tell Mary! Just wait till
I tell her! She'll fairly bust wide open."

"Slow down," I said coldly. "We'll tell Mary but that's
just the beginning. We've been living on clover. From now
on, it's dog eat dog and all the rules kicked in the river.
They won't bother about teasing us along any more, Dan.
No more playing it smooth. They'll come for us any way
they can, and I know a hundred ways. And so do they.
Maybe they know a hundred and one."

143

Dan couldn't wait for morning. He had to tell Mary before we tried to sleep. Sam growled something about "blasted women" and rode for home. Dan started for the door and said, "Say, Jim. I get the general idea of this, but what does it all mean?"

I said, "Let's walk to Mary's. I'll explain all I can on the way.".

We took the river path and I tried to give Dan a condensed lecture on railroad building and the deals that evolved behind the construction, so that a person knowing about all the bribery and tricks and under-table deals might think that the rails were only the by-product of the whole business. I was guessing about part of this, of course, but it had to go something like I told Dan:

"Railroads are built to make money," I said. "Never mind the empire-building words and the service to the nation and opening the West. A few of those men are sincere, like Hill and the Great Northern, like the men who built the Santa Fe. But remember Gould, who said he didn't build railroads, he bought them. And Fisk and others. When the first ones went across country, the government had to help the builders, or let's put it this way and say the builders were big men who knew the big politicians, and they got together and decided that the government ought to give the railroads a lot of free land on each side of the right-of-ways because the railroads were so brave and were risking so much money to build into the unknown. The result of that was, in many cases, that the big men who controlled the majority of stock in the railroad first got the land for building and then sold themselves most of the land so they could resell it for a good profit when the settlers caught up with the railroad.

"But this railroad is different, Dan. All this land was opened to the homesteaders by the passage of the homestead laws, and instead of getting free land, the railroad has to buy its right-of-way. That's all right because the landowners get a fair price, and if they try to hold up the railroad, the government forces them to sell for the fair price. But there will always be a few big men, money-hungry men, who want to line their pockets despite the laws, and they will always dig up a few possibilities to make that money. And that's what happened here, as I see it. This Northern and Western is a new company, backed by big men in the East, in St. Louis and Chicago. Now I'm not saying all of those big men are looking for easy money. But there must be one in this company who knows all about the plans and who, because he knew what would happen, came out here, or sent his men out, to find the best spot for turning those extra dollars. Now what happened?

"I think this: this big man studied all the advance surveyor and engineer reports on the planned route from Weeping Water northwest to the Green Hills, and most likely he had some of his own men on that first job to make sure. He picked this valley as the coming bread basket, the big bonanza, of the route. But he couldn't work the land grant deal because Bisonette and the ranchers were solid on the west banks, and the homesteaders were on the east bank. And there was a little trading post of a town with about thirty people, and they owned the town property and had two eyes. So what did he do? You got the answer tonight. He *lost* that first report that showed the crossing by the store was the best. He let the word get out that Blackwater was on the main line. He planned it well. Blackwater grew, of course, and this spring would find it booming and waiting for the rails. And that's when he pulled his power and had these young engineers sent out to make a last-minute security check because that old report just *happened* to turn up, and they would verify it, as you saw tonight, and there goes the railroad across at my store.

"But something went wrong. Those things have a way of sneaking out to the ears of men who look for just that kind of information. He was so sure of himself he neglected to send someone out right away to buy Simpson's land, yours, and Mr. Carr's. And while he was counting the money he'd make from selling lots in a division point town, the dam sprung a leak with no Dutch boy handy with his fat thumb. Bisonette is a big man in this state and has his ears in the state capitol. Bisonette found out. Then Mixon found out. We don't know much about him, but he saw the big chance and he hustled right out here and organized the farmers and played the good boy to cover his real purpose. And then Bisonette and Mixon, at counter-purposes and not daring to tell anyone else, hit another snag."

"Simpson," Dan said.

"Simpson," I said. "Simpson owned the key property and Bisonette controlled Simpson. But Bisonette was so sure of himself that he went too slow. Mixon showed up and scared hell out of Simpson so that Simpson was afraid to sell to Bisonette when Bisonette finally came to him. And you saw no reason to sell, and Mr. Carr wouldn't sell. I don't know if Bisonette or Mixon made a deal with the big man back East, or maybe they're both playing a lone hand. Anyway, see how luck and fate step in. Simpson was between hell and high water. Maybe he knew he'd get nothing but a bullet in the last deal—he knew too much. He sneaked out and got rid of his land to me, and disappeared. I lost my luck and came out to make a sale and then they played me wrong because time was getting short and they had to act. But think of the stake and you can see why the sky is the limit.

"In the first place, the railroad, through the conniving control of this big man, allowed everyone to think it would come through Blackwater. He knew different, as do Bisonette and Mixon. They all know that when the railroad crosses the river at my property, it will buy only right-of-way width from me and go a good distance west before it buys land for its division point yards and sidings and shops. And you can bet that big man will see that Blackwater is a division point. And that makes my land, and yours, and Mary's exactly where the new town will be. Not a little town, Dan. Weeping Water looks big to you, but it will have its day during construction and then settle back. This is the richest valley on the route. It's the natural funnel for millions of dollars' worth of future business. Think of the crops going east in the future. Grain and potatoes and fruit and fish. Think of the lumber and cattle and sheep and hogs. And the metal in the mountains—gold, silver, iron, copper, and others we don't know about yet. There's no limit. We can't visualize what the future may bring, but we can see one thing clearly now. Think of our land divided into lots for businesses and homes. You could hold onto a few or all of them, and name your own price. There is no limit to the money a man could make.

"So now we know. And they'll all know that we know in a day's time. The last hand is dealt and the stayers have drawn. This is the big pot, Dan, and they can do one of two things. They can come out in the open and buy our land, at our price, if we'll sell. Or they can kill us and throw our titles into a mess and do some bribing as only they know how, and eventually get our land. No foolishness now. It simply depends on how greedy they are. As for me, now that I know, I'll sell—at my own price. I can use the money, for a few things worthy of that money. You and Mary—you'll have to decide. But this much is sure. Until we know how they want to play the finish, we can be killed any minute of any day and night from now on."

Dan walked in silence for a few steps and then said, "It's pretty big, Jim. I didn't even guess it was like this. I'll have to talk to Mary. She's got more sense than me. Whatever she thinks, that'll be all right with me."

We turned into Mary's back yard and I said, "That's wise of you, Dan. Now let's tell her and you catch her when she faints."

Mary didn't faint. She turned very white and sat heavily in a chair and said, "I don't believe it; I simply don't believe it."

When we finally convinced her it was all true, she just shook her head and murmured, "I don't know what to do. I was worried before. Now I'm so frightened I won't sleep until something is done with this horrible land." She looked at me and said, "Jim, what are you going to do?"

I grinned. I couldn't help it, the way my thoughts were building dreams. I said, "I'll sell. At my price, and that'll be mighty big. Then I'll buy a red pony and a little rifle and a cowboy outfit with handmade boots about size five. I'll buy a little house north of town and put some good furniture in it."

Mary said, "Jim, have you lost your mind?"

"No, Mary," I said. "I've found it. That's one of the

things I'll do. Don't you like to dream about wearing fine clothes and riding in a big carriage?''

"What do you mean?'' Mary asked quickly.

"Nothing,'' I said. "I'll tell you about it later.''

Dan said, "We can get married right away. We'll buy a ranch to the west and build a big house and . . .''

"Please,'' Mary said sharply. "Don't talk like that, Dan. We haven't got all this money yet. All we have is worry, and guns, and death.''

She was worried and I decided I'd touched one of her secret dreams, or maybe she sensed that I had a good idea she was holding out on Dan for his sake. She was going to blow up in a minute. I said, "You go to bed, Mary. We'll go home and sleep on this.''

"Thank you, Jim,'' she said. "And be careful, doubly careful from now on. And go to town tomorrow and see Doc. Maybe he can tell us what to do.'' She shivered. "I'm frightened.''

I said, "All right, Mary.''

We said good night and walked back to the store. Dan said, "You want the roan in the morning?''

"No,'' I said. "I'll walk to town. You meet me at Doc's about two.''

I didn't fall asleep until almost morning, thinking about everything. Then I slept until noon.

When I started for town late that afternoon, the weather was changing. Slate-gray clouds, hanging low, were moving sullenly before a rising north wind. The sun was gone. My lungs protested against my chest, demanding more sleep. I was halfway to town when I heard the horses, and Charlotte Bisonette drew up beside me in her spring buggy. She said, "You look tired, Mr. Stanton. Won't you ride along?''

"Thank you,'' I said. "If I may.''

We didn't talk much, riding into town. Once she said,

149

"Nasty weather building," and I answered, "It's that time of year, isn't it?"

She stopped before the general store and I said, "Thank you, Miss Bisonette," and she nodded and turned away.

I moved along the sidewalk toward Doc's. Then I noticed that people were turning and watching me strangely; and at this moment, as though timed to perfection, Brent stepped from the harness shop and stood in my path. I saw Mixon's two watchdogs across the street. Then I saw Mixon in the doorway of the Granger's Rest, his bad hand still wrapped in a bandage with the small splints sticking out beyond those broken fingers, and his good hand resting lightly on his gun. His face was normal and his eyes were no longer discolored, and he watched me expectantly as though I were going to draw and fight the entire town.

Brent said, "Stanton, I reckon you better come with me."

"What for?" I asked.

"You ought to know," Brent said. "Don't start trouble, Stanton, I'm doin' my duty and not out for gunplay. I'm arresting you for the murder of Bill Higgens and you'd better come along quiet."

They hadn't wasted a moment. I stopped and looked at Brent, and along the street. They were waiting for me to make a play; they wanted me to draw. It would save them a lot of trouble. Brent was waiting, lips tight and eyes never straying from my shoulders.

God, I was a fool to walk into this. For a moment, I wanted to stop all the thinking, draw and have it out; and then I thought, that's not fair to Dan and Mary.

I fooled him. I said, "All right, Brent. I'll come along. But this is foolish."

He looked disappointed. I think he actually believed he had faced me down. He said, "Come on," and turned up the street.

I followed him to the end of the block, where the jail sat across the side street on the corner of the next block. Brent opened the office door and I followed him into a small, dirty room holding a desk, two chairs, and nothing more. He opened the big door and I saw the dirty, narrow hall with one cell on each side and a small one at the end. He opened this cell and turned on his heel.

"I'll take your guns," he said.

This was the last moment. I knew someone was standing behind me, in the doorway, waiting for a last break. I said, "Tell me one thing, Brent. How was this planned?"

"Planned?" he said. "Higgens was shot in the alley behind Doc's—with a .36 caliber bullet. Doc dug it out last night."

I drew my guns and handed them to him. He was the first man to take them that way since I got them. I said softly, "Brent, don't use those guns. Put them in your drawer for evidence and leave them alone."

That was the only soft spot in Brent. Like me, he loved his guns. He could understand my feeling. He said, "Don't worry about them, Stanton. Nobody'll use 'em until you swing. Get inside."

"Will you tell Doc I want to see him?" I asked.

"What for?"

"My rights," I said. "I want a lawyer."

Brent laughed and slammed the cell door behind me and locked it. He said, "Lawyer? You're arrested for murder, Stanton, the worst kind. A man shot in the back, a man with one hand. You'll sit here until they take you to Weeping Water to stand trial"—he grinned evilly—"or somebody tries to save the state trial money."

I said, "Get out of here, Brent. I don't want to see your face again. Yes, just one more time."

"When?" he said.

"You know when, Brent," I said. "Did you think you

made me back water? Think again, Brent. You're just a little guy working for the big ones, taking all the chances. Don't ever give me one chance, Brent.''

He wanted to laugh, and he couldn't. He said, "Cheap talk, Stanton," and closed the hall door.

I looked at my cell. It was eight by eight, maybe smaller, with a dirty cot and a wash basin and one tiny window in the rear wall, heavily barred. The jail was brick, with two-foot walls. I couldn't get out; any thought of that was foolish.

So I sat and thought and suffered. All afternoon I sat in that dirty cell, watching the sunlight poke through the west window and climb higher on the door. I tried to put myself in Mixon's place and decide on the best way to get rid of me in a hurry; and I thought of his Grangers and how far they would follow him if he pursed his lips and whistled loud and told them a good story. He could gather them in meeting and tell them that I murdered Higgens and how Bisonette and the ranchers would take this chance to show their contempt of Brent, because Brent was a Granger man, and because Higgens had run from me, by trying to get me out of jail. Oh, he would cook up something mighty good, and if he got them going, nothing in the world could stop them from marching on this pint-sized jail and stringing me to the nearest tree. I wondered dully how much those farmers knew about Mixon. I would have bet my life they had no more idea of how he had been using them to suit his own purpose than I had until the past night.

But I was happy about one thing. I had the title to my property inside my clothes, pinned to my underwear in the small of my back. They would be out at the store now, tearing it upside down, searching for that title; and eventually they would come and search me. Brent hadn't bothered with that detail; that wasn't his job. He didn't know why I was framed. So I sat there and prayed that Doc, or

Dan, or anybody, would come and help me do something that we needed desperately. And then I heard the voice.

It was a soft—"Jim!"—whisper outside the window. I leaned against the wall and said, "Who is it?"

"Red. I couldn't come till it got dark, Jim. Doc made me wait."

"Red," I said. "Tell Doc to get Dan and Mary. Hurry, Red. Don't stay there. They're watching."

He whispered, "You never done it, Jim," and he was gone.

I didn't breathe for half a minute, listening for the sound of them catching that boy. But nothing came through the cell window but the wind. It was rising now; dirty weather was building up on the Big Muddy. My chest hurt and I knew this was bad for my lungs. I buttoned my coat and turned up the collar and sat down to wait.

I heard Dan's voice first, bellowing outside the jail door, and then Brent opened the hall door and I saw them against the lamplight, Mary and Dan and Doc. Brent was saying, "All right, you can see him. But don't try nothing."

Mary said, "I want a lamp in here, Marshal."

She had dignity, even then, and Brent felt it. He mumbled, "Yes, ma'am."

He gave Dan the extra lamp and they came down the hall and stood before the cell door. Mary turned to Brent and said, "Will you please leave us alone for a few minutes?"

Brent looked at them and said, "All right," and went back to the office and shut the hall door.

I said, "Is Red all right?"

"Fine," Doc said softly. "He's at my place, Jim."

Dan said, "I'll get you out, Jim. Just wait a little while."

"Don't talk like that," Mary snapped. "Jim, we know you didn't shoot Higgens. Doc knows it."

"A nice job," Doc said softly. His round face was angry

in the yellow light. He said, "Jim, I've taken no sides since I hit this town. I now declare myself on your side of the fence."

"Thanks, Doc," I said quickly. "Now, turn around, Mary. I'll get the title. Dan, you got yours?"

"Right here," Dan whispered.

Mary turned and I stripped down and unpinned the envelope, got back in my clothes, and unfolded the title. I said, "Doc, do you know the laws on title and deed in this state? We've got to deed our property to Mary, right now, and do it legally. How many witnesses does it take?"

"One," Mary said. "Doc can witness both of them. I've got pen and ink in my purse."

"Good girl," I said. "Hurry now."

Mary opened her leather purse and Doc held the ink bottle and the pen. Mary had two blank quitclaim deeds and she unfolded these and flattened them against Dan's back and said, "One dollar makes it legal, Jim. I will give you and Dan a dollar each. Doc will witness it. We'll sign these deeds and Dan and I will ride to Weeping Water tomorrow and register them at the courthouse. Doc, have I forgotten anything?"

"No," Doc said softly. "But hurry up."

I took one blank deed and read it quickly; and then we filled in the blanks and signed our names. It read like this:

"Know all men by these presents, that I, Jim Stanton, of Blackwater, in the County of Weeping Water and State of ———, in consideration of the sum of one dollar received to my full satisfaction of Mary Carr, the receipt therof I do hereby acknowledge, have and do hereby freely remise, release and forever QUITCLAIM unto the said Mary Carr, her heirs and assigns, all my right, title, interest, or demand, in or unto a certain piece of land, the southeast quarter of section forty-two (42) in the Township of Blackwater, County of Weeping Water, and State of ———, containing one hundred and sixty acres, more or less, according to the United States surveys.

To Have and To Hold the above granted and bargained premises, with the privileges thereunto belonging, to the said Mary Carr, her heirs and assigns, to her and their own proper use, benefit and behoof forever.

In Witness Whereof, I have hereunto set my hand and seal this fourth day of November, in the year of our Lord one thousand eight hundred and seventy-five.

Jim Stanton (seal)

Signed, sealed and delivered
   in the presence of
  Charles Nichols
State of ———   ss.
Weeping Water County

Personally appeared this fourth day of November, A.D. 1875, Jim Stanton, the signer and sealer of the above written instrument, and acknowledged the same to be his free act and deed, before me.''

I said, "Mary, you've got to have a justice of the peace or some county official sign this at the bottom to make it legal. Do you know anyone in Weeping Water who'll help us out?"

"Yes," Mary said. "An old friend of my father's, a judge. He'll help. Hurry, Dan. Sign your name."

Mary folded the deeds and slipped them inside her dress, and the pen and ink disappeared into her purse, and we stood innocently on each side of the cell door. That was a relief.

I said, "Mary, you stay in Weeping Water with that judge. Have you got enough money?"

She just nodded, looking at me.

"Stop worrying," I said. "They can't touch you, Mary. And they'll have to take me to Weeping Water for trial, and then we'll blow the lid off this business so everybody in the state knows what someone is trying to do. Doc, when does court meet again?"

"In session now," Doc said. "Don't worry, they'll . . ." he stopped and coughed, and went on, "They'll try you soon, Jim."

I knew why he stopped talking. He almost said, "They'll never try you if the big boy can stop you. You'll get lynch law or shot on the road."

Mary said, "Jim—what can I . . . ?"

"Go home," I said. "Get your sleep. Dan, it's you and Doc and Sam now. Get her to Weeping Water."

Dan said, "Don't worry, Jim. We'll take care of you. I been fiddling around long enough. You say the word and I'll rip this place apart right now."

"No," I said. "That's what they want. Let's sit tight and see what happens."

"I'll be near," Doc said gently. "You need a blanket or two, Jim? It's turning cold."

"I've got two here," I said. "I'll be fine. Now get started, for God sakes."

They all looked at me and then went through the big door and into the night. Brent slammed the outside door and stuck his head through the hall door and grinned at me.

"Feel better now?" he called.

"Sure," I said.

"That's good," he said. "They're talking it up in the saloons, Stanton. And I've only got one deputy. I better go out and swear in a few more. But don't let that bother you. Get a good night's sleep."

I said, "You can kindly go to hell, Brent," and turned my back on him.

I felt better now. I sat down on the bunk and wrapped the blankets around me, and almost broke my promise and called out for a cigar. Mary had the titles and deeds, all clear and legal, and if they did get me and figured they could run a fast one and bring in a ringer to take possession as a distant relative, after my unfortunate death, they would be rudely jolted. There was some satisfaction in that, I thought, and I would also make sure that Dan took care of Red and his mother; and if Dan didn't make it, well, Mary would do anything I told her. She was a wonderful woman.

It was an hour or so before midnight when I heard faint voices. The wind was howling now and I knew snow was falling outside, but how thickly I could not tell through the small window. I hoped the storm would hold off, or be light enough for Dan and Mary to get through to Weeping Water in the morning. The voices trickled through that closed hall door between windblasts. I decided it must be Brent and his deputy blabbing in the office, and then the hall door opened and I saw Brent walk stiffly toward my cell with someone close behind him.

I said, "Let a man sleep, Brent."

Brent didn't say a word. He bent down and fumbled with his keys and unlocked the cell door and pulled it open. Then I saw her standing behind him with a .44 lined on his back.

She said, "Hurry, Jim!"

It was the first time she'd called me Jim. I stood there and finally I said, "Charlotte! How . . ."

"Don't talk," she said. "Tie this scoundrel up and stick a bar down his throat."

I hesitated, wondering if this was a deadfall, a trick to

get me outside and shoot me down. I said, "Who's with you?"

"Don't worry about that," she said. "Tie him up."

"How'd you know?" I asked.

"Red," she said. "Doc. Hurry, Jim!"

I looked quickly at Brent and decided when I saw his face. He wasn't an actor and he wasn't faking his fear. His face was yellow and slack. This was no deadfall. I didn't ask her why, or for what reason, but my mind leaped out of that dirty cell and raced far ahead. I could tell Mary and Dan, then hide out in the Cup with Sam until things shaped up. That was better than lying in jail, waiting for a lynch mob or a crooked trial, and besides, I did want to live.

"Right with you," I said. "Get in here, Brent."

I pushed him into the cell and tripped him. He flailed out with his arms and I slugged him across the neck and he went down on his face beside the bunk. Charlotte said, "Here," and tossed me a length of rope. I tied and gagged him so thoroughly it would take five men ten minutes to cut him loose and find his tongue. Then I stepped into the hall and closed the cell door, locked it, and followed Charlotte into the office.

Clancy was standing against the outside door with a double-barreled shotgun, holding Brent's deputy frozen in a chair against the far wall. The deputy was ready to die with benefit of gunshot. Clancy grinned at me and jerked his head toward the desk.

"Your guns are in the drawer," he said. "Hurry up."

I found my guns, checked them, and held them at my sides. I said, "Now what?"

"Cover this gent," Clancy said, "I'll hogtie him."

Clancy's tie job made mine look like the work of a child. That deputy couldn't move when Clancy yanked his last half-hitch tight and rolled the stiff form under the desk. I went to the window and peeked through the crack between drawn green shade and casing, and saw nothing. It was snowing hard.

I said, "How did you know?"

Charlotte said, "I saw Brent take you in. I went straight to Doc"—she smiled—"we're better friends than you knew, Jim. Little Red was there. He saw Brent shoot his father in the alley behind Doc's last night."

"The gun?" I said. "Another .36?"

"It's gone," Charlotte said. "And so are we. They're going to lynch you tonight, Jim. All the farmers in the valley came to town after they took you in. Mixon's two toughs are in the Granger's Rest, buying free drinks and heating them up. Brent was going to step aside and let them walk right in and take you." She smiled bitterly. "Courtesy of our friend, Mr. Mixon, I am sure."

"Stop dallyin'," Clancy said. "Come on."

She must have driven all the way home, I thought, to get these men and come back to help me. To help me? I was confused. I tried to reason it out and Clancy opened the door an inch and looked down Main. He said, "Nice snow, let's go," and lit out and across the side streets to the alley that ran between Doc's and Mrs. Higgen's house. We ran down the alley and Clancy said, "In the woodshed," and we ducked into Doc's woodshed which set flush on the alley. Doc spoke from the darkness.

"Jim?"

"Here," I said. "Thanks to Charlotte and Clancy."

"Brent?" Doc lashed out with an unexpected savageness.

"He'll keep," Clancy drawled. "The boss'll hit town in an hour with every man from the hills."

I said, "Charlotte, why . . . ?"

"Doc told me everything," Charlotte said. "Dan told him when he left you at the jail. Jim, why didn't you believe my father? He knows nothing about the railroad changing its route. He doesn't care about land and towns and making that sort of money that way. He was completely honest with you, Jim, when he told you why he wanted your land. He didn't trust Mixon and he hates to have people too close to him. When I told him, he sent me back with Clancy and five men. He's getting every rancher and man in the hills to help.''

"Charlotte," I said. "Will you forgive me?"

I know she smiled in the darkness because her hand came out and touched my arm. She said, "Of course, Jim. You're like my father, underneath. It just takes a little while to know you."

"Doc," I said. "It's Mixon. Mixon all the way and fronting for somebody as big as they come."

"Well," Doc said dryly. "I suggest you use the extra horse these good people just happened to bring along, and stop at Mary's and tell her, and then get Dan and join your friend with the long rifle down in the Cup. Sam knows a hundred ways in and out, and we can always get word to you through Bisonette. Let the town cool off overnight. Bisonette and his friends will be here soon and take care of our friend, Marshal Brent. These farmers will find their fatted calf flown, and they'll have to stay in town tonight because of the storm, and come morning when they hear Red's side of the story, they'll do some straight thinking and everything will be all right. In the meantime, you're safest with old Sam and Dan, down in the Cup."

"Another thing," Charlotte said. "Why not take Mary to our place? She'll be safer there."

Things were looking bright again. I said, "We'll do that. She'd be safer than in Weeping Water. And the titles with her." I laughed then. "Maybe we'll have some fun with that big boy yet, Doc."

"Time to figure later," Doc said. "Start riding."

I remembered one more thing; and it was the sad part of

this whole business. I said, "Doc, tell Red I'll see him soon. And for him and his mother not to worry about anything. You tell him that, Doc."

"Why," Doc said gently. "I don't need to, Jim. Red's been telling that himself, ever since he came from the jail. He says you'll look out for him, and shoot Brent for killing his father."

"Yes," I said. "That pigeon is all mine."

We pulled off the road just north of Mary's, riding in thick falling snow that already blanketed the ground. I couldn't see six feet and the horses made no sound. I cupped my hand against Charlotte's ear and said, "Get under the trees and keep awake. I'll go around in back. They might be watching. If you hear a shot, come boiling."

She nodded and reached over to poke Clancy, and they rode to the west and vanished before I turned toward the river.

This was an early storm and certainly early snow. I hoped it wouldn't turn into a blizzard. I knew those sudden, vicious storms and what they did to this country. I walked slowly, holding my right gun free under my coat and brushing snow from my face, trying to keep my bearings and come around on the house.

I felt, rather than saw, her back gate. It was open. I stopped then, straining my ears, waiting for some sound. Only the wind and the snow. I went through the gate and advanced on the house, one step at a time, bringing both guns out now and clasping them cross-armed under my armpits to keep them dry. I reached the stone patio around her back door and my boots made a soft "shuff-shuff" through the snow. I waited a minute then, looking all around, and moved onto the porch. I wondered when they would find Brent and his deputy. Time was a precious metal to me then.

The door stood ajar and I swallowed hard, fearing something I couldn't name, and then I saw the lamp shining, a tiny beam cattycornered through the curtain crack in the kitchen window. I slammed the door back and leaped into the kitchen.

It was empty; the fire in the stove was burning low and the house was getting cold. I went into the frontroom. The house was small; it had one bedroom, kitchen, and a big living room. The kitchen wasn't upset and the big room was neat and clean, just as she always kept it. I was frantic now. I stepped into her bedroom, and then I looked at the floor beside the bed and over by the closet, which was closed, and I knew.

I was sick for a moment. I felt everything go out of my heart and die on the floor.

She was gone, and that purse was gone, too; also her heavy fur coat and cap.

The bedroom was cold and snow hadn't melted on the floor; it lay where they had tracked it in and lost it in gobs and boot marks. I could see the big tracks where a man had stood beside the bed and helped her pack a few pieces of clothing, where he held the closet door while she dressed in her fur coat and cap. I even thought I could read those snow tracks where she turned and went on tiptoe to kiss him. I saw those big tracks and I remembered a hot morning in the dusty yard before the store and how I could still see the gouges made by those big round-headed cleats. They were plain on the floor to me, the same holes in the loose snow and beside the closet, on the floor, where they had dug small, sliver-edged channels in that clean, well-kept floor.

Not Dan. Not big-hearted, trusting, courageous Dan, but Mixon!

Now I saw that it had been Mixon all the time, Mixon and Mary. It was all coming clear.

I thought of the bread she couldn't bake, and the fine but faded clothes she wore, and how she had enough money when the farm wasn't bringing in that much. I opened the closet door and saw her clothes on their neat hangers, the fine dresses and shirts and underthings she didn't wear outside; the few fine things she had to keep hidden in her closet because she had vanity and money, and she had to put them on late at night, for a few minutes, to feed herself on that vanity and keep going; and probably count her money and feel the satisfaction of knowing there was more, all she wanted, whenever she needed it. I looked down at the two pair of beautiful little shoes for her shapely feet, and a pair of kid boots made in New York.

Kid boots for a farm girl?

It was all there and I'd been taken so smoothly, so wonderfully, I never felt pressure, I never knew the pain until now.

I didn't have time to look any more, but I didn't have to. I went through the house and out the front door to the road. I was thinking it all out now, putting the pieces together and wondering, even then, how I could tell Dan.

She had gotten him to go home, tonight of all nights, and he was there, waiting for morning, trusting her completely.

I found Charlotte and Clancy in the trees across the road. The wind had risen now and snow was slashing along the ground, beating against my face. I noticed that five more riders stood behind them. Charlotte had really been ready for action.

I mounted the horse and pulled in between them. I had to shout now, to make them hear. I told them as simply as possible and Clancy swore harshly. Charlotte turned, her face deep in her turned-up fur collar, and shouted back:

"I won't say I knew it all the time, Jim. I just thought she was too proud."

I said, "We'll go to Dan's."

It was tough riding even that far. We passed my store and I saw only its faint bulk through the falling snow, and when we reached Dan's front yard I rode my horse up to the door and hammered on it with my stirrup. I heard him move cautiously and I shouted, "Dan, open up!"

"My God!" he roared. "Jim!"

He almost tore his door off the hinges, pulling it open. I got down and told Clancy to take the horses to the lee side of the house. Then I went inside and brushed the snow off and told him.

He wanted to shoot me before I got halfway through. When I finished talking he turned away and walked into the kitchen and we stood in his big room and looked at each other and waited. There was nothing we could do. I knew he'd be all right. I had faith in him; faith in his belief in everything that was good and clean and honest.

He came back after a minute and licked his big, wide mouth and gave Charlotte a smile of thanks. I saw her eyes on him, and then I knew something else that Dan had never discovered.

"They must be riding for Weeping Water," Dan said hoarsely. "I only left her place an hour ago. That means Mixon was out back all the time. She made me ride home on the road."

"Can they make it?" I asked Clancy. "In this storm?"

"Sure," Clancy said. "They'll have to ride easy but they can warm up at the halfway station. I'd say about fifteen hours' riding, Jim, give or take a little."

"But we can't catch them," Charlotte said. "We can't ride any faster than they."

I was thinking of Brent, back in town, and how those farmers would act when they found him, after Bisonette's crowd moved in and told them the truth; and I tried to think this out and could not find a way. We were licked if we didn't catch Mixon and Mary.

I said, "We've got to get them before they make Weeping Water."

Clancy shook his head morosely.

"We can make a try," Dan said suddenly, looking up and slamming his big hands together.

"With horses?" Clancy said. "No chance, Dan."

"Not horses," Dan said. "The river!"

"The river?" I asked stupidly.

"Sam's canoe," Dan said. "We'll ride to his place and take his canoe. The river makes its bend and runs close to the road about ten miles this side of Weeping Water. Don't you remember, Jim, when you came with Henry? Don't stand there. Let's go!"

I turned to Charlotte and said, "It's a chance. We'll take it. You can help on this end."

She said, "How?"

"Meet your father and his men at the store," I said. "Clancy, you take five men and get the best horses and start for Weeping Water. We'll meet you somewhere on the road. Charlotte, tell your father about Mary, about the things he doesn't know. Tell him to take the town. Don't let Brent get away. Keep him in jail and have his guns ready for him. I'll depend on you and your father and Doc to tell those farmers what happened. And wait for us. We should see you tomorrow afternoon, pretty late"—I tried to smile—"if we're still kicking."

She looked at Dan and she didn't bat an eye with worry you could see, the kind of half-hidden, sweetly pathetic worry Mary used to let us see, as if she were being brave. She said, "We'll see you then."

She ran for the door with Clancy following, and they were riding for town before we buttoned up. There was a girl, I thought, who had fooled me as badly one way as Mary had the other.

I said then: "Dan, have we got a chance?"

"Fair," Dan said. "Don't think about it. Just ride."

We went outside and headed south. We had the advantage here; we were moving with the wind and the snow at our backs, and when we bored deeper into the Cup, the trees and canyons would break the wind and drop the snow slow and straight. We had fifteen miles to ride, and then the river with a canoe, and I knew nothing about canoes and rivers; and pile a storm and snow and darkness on top of fast running water, with three men in a small canoe, and the chances are mighty bad. But we had to do it. I scrooched down in my coat and bent in the saddle and rode.

Seven

I WAS RIDING IN THE SOFT CENTER OF NOTHINGNESS WITH a weight on my shoulders and my lungs hurting spasmodically; and I swayed in this velvety bed suspended between ground and sky, and decided it was foolish to stand when all I had to do was relax and let myself fall forever into the soft whiteness my eyes saw around me. I was falling from the saddle when Dan's voice roared in my ear, "Just made it," and the floating movement stopped and I felt Dan's big arms lifting me to the ground.

"Sam's?" I asked.

"Walk," Dan called. "Keep walking, Jim."

I was dizzy and I remembered nothing about our ride into the Cup. Dan guided me to the door and hammered it with his fist and called, "Sam . . . Sam!" and the door came open at once and I saw the lamp and the hairy, scrawny arm behind the lamp, and then my eyes threw off their mist and I could see Sam's face in the dancing yellow lamplight.

"You crazy?" Sam said. "Git in here."

Dan helped me inside and I sat on the bench before the fireplace while Sam built a huge, quick blaze that melted the snow on my hat and coat before I could strip them off and hold out my hands to that heat. Sam said, "I'll bed the horses," and went outside to lead them around to the stable. Dan stamped his feet and waved this arms, kicking snow from his boots and slapping it off his clothes. I sat down again in front of the fire and moved my hands and feet, and felt the warmth creep into my body. Sam came from the stable and moved around the cabin, and then I saw the bottle thrust under my nose.

I murmured, "Can't, Sam."

Sam growled, "This is different. Drink!"

It was pure corn whisky and it brought me to my feet, gagging and gaining the false strength of liquor. I walked around the cabin three times, took another drink, and said, "Tell him, Dan. I'd better rest."

I felt my lungs pushing against my chest, aching and throbbing and I decided it was foolish to do anything according to the rules. I took another short drink and grabbed Sam's tobacco and papers from the table and built a smoke while Dan told him what had happened. The smoke went down my throat and into my lungs, and I coughed and blew it out, and tried again. This time it stayed down. I smoked that one to a nub and had a second one going like the fire when Dan finished.

"Good thinkin'," Sam said then. "We'd best git started. Jim, you need more duds."

"Don't worry about me," I said. "I'm all right."

Sam said, "Sure, sure," and made me put on a heavy wool shirt and a buckskin jacket under my coat, and wrap a big fur scarf around my head and jam my hat down tightly over the scarf. He gave me a pair of fur mittens that allowed my fingers room to curl and clench, and did away with the stiffness a man is bound to get in common finger gloves. Dan buttoned up and Sam slipped into buckskins and a heavy blue blanket coat and the same kind of head scarf and mittens. They both took a long drink from the

bottle and offered me another. I said, "Enough," and Sam
grinned at me and got a short repeating rifle from the wall
and a blanket to cover the rifles in the canoe, and they
were ready.

I followed them down the path to the river and waited
while they carried the canoe from a lean-to under the trees
and placed it gently, carefully, in the water beside the dock.
Down here, where the wind was masked by the canyon
walls, snow fell straight and thick but a man could see
objects at ten feet. I stared at that canoe and if I hadn't
been desperate, nothing on God's beautiful green earth
would have gotten me into such a frail craft. Or so it
looked; for I learned differently.

"You in the bow, Jim," Sam said. "Dan in the middle,
me in the stern. Jim, you watch for snags and loose logs.
Me and Dan'll paddle."

They steadied the canoe and I stepped gingerly from the
dock and found myself sitting low and fairly comfortable
in the bow. Dan's great weight dropped gently amidships
and Sam stepped lightly into the stern and pushed us away
from the dock toward midstream. I felt the current tug at
the canoe. We were in the river, on our way. Sam called,
"Easy like, Dan boy," and I felt their paddles bite the
water. Then I huddled down in the bow and peered ahead.

The canoe was a sixteen footer, built by Sam, with certain ideas of his lovingly worked into its frame. It was
wider than most canoes and the sides curved out and then
came around in almost a flat bottom, called a whale-bottom
by some people I knew, so that we rode fairly high and
steadier than an ordinary canoe. It was drum-tight, I found,
for we shipped not an ounce of water through its skin; and
only the snow drifting between us wet the inside.

It is impossible now, with that ride behind me, to re-
count all that happened with any clarity. I know that the
river was running black and fast before me and around me,

water gurgling on each side of the bow and snow falling thickly, a pale white blanket encompassing the earth and water. I could not see the canyon walls, but high above us, the free wind moaned and slatted through the trees growing along the canyon edges; and when we passed the mouths of ravines leading into the canyon, gusts of that wind would curl out across the river, tossing the water high and pasting our backs and faces with the thick, wet snow. My fingers were clutching the rail so tightly they went numb within the fur mittens and I had to open them, one finger at a time, like an old man getting up in the morning, and hold them close to my chest to warm them. I was crouching on my knees, doubled down on the backs of my lower legs, my upper body bent forward in the bow so my eyes were just level with the bow, giving me all the view ahead I needed. I could not see more than ten feet, and that no more than a merging, then wavering, mass of black water and white snow.

Sam steered us to midstream where the current was moving with deceptive swiftness; I felt it tug and snarl at the canoe and then accept the burden and take us in its liquid arms and hurl us downstream, blind and hoping. Sam and Dan paddled, one on each side, not fast but with a steady pull-lift-pull-lift, that I felt in the vibration of the canoe as their work and the current sent us shooting to the south.

My mind soared away from the canoe and seemed to spin and cry in a garbled frenzy of conflicting thoughts. I began to estimate time. I'd been up since noon and that was twelve hours, maybe more, and I'd had less than six hours' sleep the night before. That's nothing, I told myself. I'd stayed up three days and nights once in a big game. Nothing, the river seemed to gurgle thickly. Wait till you play me for a few hours, Stanton.

I went over the night and remembered when Mary and Dan left the jail, when Charlotte and her father's men got me out of jail, when I saw Doc, when we rode south of Mary's house and I learned the truth about her, when we went on to Dan's and I saw him battle over what I had to tell him. I realized then, looking back, that Dan had always been the one who offered affection to Mary; and Mary was always calm and cool, never giving him a great deal in return. But how could she when she had the face of a madonna and the heart of a snake.

How fast would Mixon and Mary ride, how fast would they push horses through the storm? Would they rest at the halfway house and change to fresh horses? How many miles of river did we have ahead before we reached the road? How fast was this river running and did it slow down when we swung to the east, and it widened? Of course it did; it had to. That was a fact any child knew. Compress water; you get rapids, falls, swift-running current; give it more room, wider banks, with the same volume of water, and you had slow-running current. How may hours till dawn? Would the snow stop?

I wanted to turn and shout at Dan and Sam, ask them these questions and be calmed and encouraged by them. But that was foolish. I would get my face wet and I might miss a snag in the water. Not that it made any difference, I realized then. We were moving too rapidly for me to see something from ten feet, shout a warning, and expect them to swerve the canoe. That was when I knew how much they cared, how their courage was something to value and keep forever. If we went over out here—I put that out of my mind. We couldn't; it wasn't in the books.

So we went in the storm and night, and we came out of the canyon and moved between low hills on a wider river. I felt the current slack and grow rougher. The wind had a clear shot at us now; it howled across the water, tossing it, rocking us, flinging snow with no form or pattern. This was the miserable part of the ride; I was covered with wet snow in a matter of moments. Behind me, Dan grunted and rested a moment, and then dug in again. He was tireless; he'd been paddling since we left Sam's dock. He paddled on; he didn't stop more than half a minute at any time.

I do not remember when we made the broad sweeping turn to the east; but snow began slapping against the left side of my face and I pulled the fur scarf forward on that side and yanked my hat at an angle to protect my cheek and nose from the wind and snow; and then I knew we had made the turn and were moving almost due east. That was the moment we missed the tree by inches.

I saw its water-logged, black hulk moving toward us from the east, the wind pushing it into and against the current so that it was gradually moving across and down the river. I will never forget how it looked, in the split-second I saw it, with the torn roots sticking out in a hundred curling shapes and prongs and how it rolled sluggishly and sucked low in the black water. I know I yelled and felt the canoe leap under me.

We passed it so closely that I felt one root end touch and run its finger along the side of the canoe, and then we were past and running into nothingness again; and behind me, Dan let out a great whoosh of air and shouted, "Never get closer to hell, Jim."

I silently agreed and huddled lower in the bow, turning my body a little to the right, away from the wind and driving snow.

Dawn was announced early by a lessening of the wind and snow. This happened suddenly, it seemed to me, for one moment I was cringing from the steady slap-slap of snow striking my head and shoulder and the next it was a gentle pat-pat and the wind had lost its bite. Sam called from the stern: "No snow by dawn."

"How far?" I shouted.

"Little way," Dan roared. "We'll have light soon."

Six o'clock now, I thought. That makes eighteen hours without sleep. And nothing like that poker game. This was harder on a man than all the poker games in his lifetime, stacked one on the other.

Now I could see farther across the river. The banks loomed into visibility before my eyes, smudged along the water's edge with ragged black streaks where the water melted the snow and carried it downstream, and dull white mounds that rose in layers from this black edge toward the white hills. The sky was a dirty gray and I saw no light in the east to mark a sunrise. The sun could be rising in the west for any difference in that gray mask across the sky. And then it was a gray morning over a white land, with the hills rolling away to the north and south and the river racing blackly before us into the east. I rubbed my eyes and stared north, trying to pick out a landmark, find a clue to give me a position. It was useless. I'd been over that road once, and then in early fall, and snow can change country completely.

Dan called, "Close now, Sam."

"Keep paddlin'," Sam answered. "Put your back to it, Dan."

We seemed to leap forward and glide along the river, and the snow was a soft falling mist, dropping nearly straight downward as the wind died away. Sam was right. This storm had shot its wild bolt during the night and would be gone by early morning. We flew down-river with both of them paddling swiftly now, digging their blades deep and following through to the last moment before they lifted and moved forward to dig in again.

It was about six o'clock or a little after. Somewhere to the north, riding on that rough road, were two people I wanted to see, face to face, more than I cared for an extra ten years of life. I had never considered killing a woman; now I didn't know. I realize now that I was so tired and

173

nervous and filled with black anger that anything seemed possible to me. As for Mixon—I wanted to place twelve rounds in his chest and watch him drop and die at my feet. I was almost at the limit of my endurance and patience—almost.

Sam called, "We'll move in," and changed course.

I could see nothing to the north; no sign of a road. We moved against the current and slipped into slack water, and then the bow ground through a thin film of shore ice and we hit the bank. Dan leaped past me and stood spraddled out on the slippery mud, holding the bow while Sam eased the stern against the bank. Sam stepped ashore and they gave me their hands and lifted me to solid ground. Dan tried to grin and showed his teeth through his snow-caked face.

"Can you lug the rifles?" he asked.

I nodded and shouldered their rifles and they lifted the canoe and carried it up the bank. I followed, sliding and falling to my knees in deep, wet snow. We climbed this sloping bank and stood on a level spot above the river and below a long ridge. They laid the canoe on the upper side of the level spot, finding two short pieces of log and turning the canoe bottom up on these logs. Then Sam took his rifle, rubbed it reflectively, and said, "Road's a mile north, over the ridge. You figure it that way, Dan?"

"Right at a mile," Dan said. "We better move."

The walk was worse than the river ride, in some respects. I was stiff and cold, and my head ached and my lungs were white fire. They knew I was nearly gone and they got on each side of me and held my arms, and we plowed up that endless ridge in foot-deep snow. It was bad going. My boots were wet and my toes slogged inside my wet socks and the water ran from heel to toe with each step. We would plunge one leg into snow and move up the ridge and hit a hole and go hip deep; and once I fell before they grabbed me and they had to brush me off. But we made the ridge top and went down the other side, and stopped in the bottom for a blow.

"Road," Sam said, pointing.

Then I could see the line of its passage around the hill to our north. It came from the east and made this wide sweeping turn along the curve of the hill, and I faintly remembered that here was where he had started to climb as we left the river on my ride from Weeping Water.

We made it to the road and I leaned against a rock and got my breath and stared at the snow. Dan peered along the surface of the road and looked at Sam. He said, "Did they beat us, Sam?"

"Nope," Sam said. "Nary a track. And no dips."

I knew vaguely what Sam meant. If they had ridden past, it couldn't have been much before dawn, and if the last hour of snow had covered their tracks, it would have shown the depression of their horses' hoof holes. The road was smooth and white. We'd made a good race. I looked at Dan.

He said, "How do we do this, Jim?"

"I want them alive," I said, reason returning now and rationalizing my anger. "I want to take them back to Blackwater and get this business squared around. I want them to see Brent and everyone in this. We'll get it out of them."

"Alive?" Dan said. "Him?"

"I want him alive to take back," I said. "After that, he's all yours. Right now, just leave him whole enough to walk or ride."

That satisfied Dan. He turned and said, "Sam, where do we cover up?"

"On the hilltop," Sam said. "We can hunker down and let 'em come to us. They'll be blowin' hard from climbin' the other side. We won't have much trouble." He gave us a wintry stare. "You say no killin', Jim. I reckon I better tell you—if that Mixon makes a move, I won't exactly kill him but he won't be healthy for a good spell."

"If you have to," I said. "Use your own judgment, Sam."

"Here," Dan said. "Grab my arm, Jim. You're ready to fold."

Sam placed us at the hilltop. The road made its curve and dropped away into the valley between this hill and the next one to the northwest, and it was a nice long climb from the bottom to where we sat on both sides of the road. Sam placed me between two boulders on the right side of the road, which was the high side. I sat back comfortably with my back against the jutting end of the big boulder, and had a clear view down the road and to the opposite hilltop. Dan was across from me behind a hump of earth and snow. Sam had gone down the hill about twenty paces and disappeared between rocks. His plan was a good one because he'd let them pass him and when they reached the top, between Dan and me, Dan would tell them to hold up and if Mixon made a move Sam would let him have a shot past his head from behind. That would discourage any gunplay. I doubted that Mixon would try a break, caught as he would be, cold and stiff from his ride.

Dan called to me, "You all right, Jim?"

"Fine," I said. "My feet act like they might belong to my body again."

"Shut up," Sam's voice floated softly from downhill. "No more talkin'. Words carry on cold air."

So we didn't talk. We sat and waited and day came gray and then dirty white, and finally as clear as it would get under those clouds. It was cold and clear and quiet. Very quiet.

I saw them come over the hill to the northwest. That was an hour later. Mixon was riding ahead and Mary in

his trail. They moved slowly against the background of
white snow, two black dots edging carefully down the in-
visible white road. It seemed an eternity before they reached
the bottom and stopped a moment, and then urged their
horses toward us, up the long grade. Mary was now in the
lead and Mixon rode a few paces behind her, turning his
head every ten feet or so to shade an arm over his eyes and
stare at the horizon. Worried, I thought, not sure of himself
even when he holds four aces in the game.

I flexed my fingers in the heavy mittens and was satisfied. They were warm and loose again. I judged distance
and pulled off the mittens and stuffed them in my pocket
and drew both guns. I held them between my legs, keeping
my hands warm, and waited.

They were halfway up the hill, then almost to the top. I
could see Mary's face deep in her fur cap and coat collar,
the calm, cool mouth and eyes. Nothing disturbed her very
much, I thought. What a superb actress. Oh, more than that!
Then they were fifty yards, thirty, ten, and they passed Sam.

They reached the top and Mixon said, "Hold up, Mary,"
and they paused while their horses snorted and quivered
with cold, breath white-plumed against the gray sky. Mixon raised both hands to adjust his cap and Dan's voice
came, deep and sharp, from the other side of the road.

"Keep them right there, Mixon."

She didn't believe her ears. She jerked her head toward
the sound and her hands fluttered on the saddle horn and
started toward her coat pocket. Mixon froze in place, hands
on his cap.

I said, "Keep your hands out, Mary."

Mixon said, "Ahhh," and wanted to draw, and Sam
shot, the sound clear and flat, and the bullet passed between them. Sam's voice floated uphill:

"Never shot me a gal yet. Sure don't want to start now—
unless I have to."

That finished them. They didn't move a muscle.

I said, "Raise your arms above your heads—hurry up!"

They did. I got up and stepped into the road, and Dan came from the downhill side, his rifle on them. I said, "Hold their horses, Dan."

He caught both bridles, and I said, "Get down, with your arms up."

Mixon just slipped off the back of his horse. Mary looked at me warmly, thankfully, and said, "I don't understand, Jim. He made me . . ."

"Get down," I said.

I reached up and caught her belt and pulled her off the horse. She fell at my feet and I boosted her up, opened her coat, and took the small derringer from her inside jacket pocket, and pulled a .36 caliber London Navy Colt from her fur coat outer pocket. I wondered how much time and trouble it had taken to get that gun for one small scene in the play. I went around to Mixon and felt him up and down, both sides, and took his .44, and a short knife from a sheath behind his neck. That was the size of their artillery; they hadn't expected any trouble. But the Navy Colt! She was more than careful. She didn't leave any evidence behind.

Sam came up the road behind them and looked at Mixon. He spat and said, "Yellowbelly," and didn't bother to look at Mary.

She was thinking fast and she looked at me appealingly. She didn't look at Dan. She said, "Jim, he forced me to come along."

"Well, now," I said softly. "In that case he'll have the titles and deeds on him, won't he, Mary? They being the thing we're all mighty concerned over."

She said, "Please, Jim?"

"Don't beg," I said. "It doesn't become you, Mary. Just give me those titles and the deeds."

She didn't move. I said, "All right, I'll undress you right here and tear your clothes apart till I find them."

She stared at me and said, "You would, wouldn't you, you filthy, sick-lunged beast!"

"The titles," I said. "Now."

I slapped her face. I meant to make it hard, and it was. It knocked her spinning against her horse and brought some sense into her head. She opened her jacket and handed me a flat wallet. I opened it and found Dan's title and deed, and my title and deed. I said, "Where's your title, Mary?"

She laughed. "Not here, Jim, I'll keep that much."

"Will you now?" I said. I turned to Mixon. "On you?"

Mixon shook his head. He had gotten over his surprise and now he stood, big and tense, but afraid at last. He was a good man in a bad way, I thought, and what a waste of a life.

I said, "We'll talk a little. I don't know all the facts but I can guess. But I want to know one thing right now. Who shot Higgens with this .36?"

"Ah, hell!" Mixon said gruffly. "This thing is busted wide open. Who do you think, Stanton?"

"I know," I said. "Brent. It took a stupid fool like Brent, working for you, Mixon. I'll even wager he knew nothing about Mary."

"That's enough, Tom," Mary said curtly. "They can't touch us."

Mixon glanced at Dan and laughed. "My dear," he said, "you wanted it this way and you say they can't touch us. Use your head, Mary. They can do whatever they like with us."

I said, "Do you want to tell me the story, or wait till we get back to Blackwater?"

Mixon didn't like that. He said, "Let's strike a deal. How much for your land, both of you, now you know what it's worth?"

"No deal," I said. "We're going back, Mixon. Things will be a little different in town when your trusting farmers hear about this. I think we'll just toss you in that dirty jail after Brent sings his song, if he hasn't already, which I am inclined to doubt, because Bisonette has taken over the town. Brent did the shooting but you hired him, Mixon, and Mary ordered you. That'll take care of both of you. That'll bust things wide open."

They had no choice. Mixon said, "What do you want?"

Mary said, "Tom . . ."

"Shut up!" Mixon said. "I did the work and lost the pot. You stand to lose nothing you haven't got."

Mixon told us what we wanted to know; it was, for all the time and money and energy expended, quite simple. Mary's father was the big boy in the railroad. Not an active member, as they call them, but the majority stockholder. He read the first reports and saw the opportunity in Blackwater and the valley. He had employed Mixon before, in the South and East. He brought Mary, who was certainly a chip off the old block, along with him and bought the farm. He tried to buy Simpson but Simpson was under Bisonette's thumb. Mary made Dan fall in love with her, and Mixon organized his Grangers and did his job well. Then Mary's father vanished, as planned, and Mary made certain the valley knew about the trouble. Mixon prodded Bisonette and Bisonette reacted as expected. Everything was going fine until Simpson ran away and I turned up with the title to that key property. Then they had to change a few plans.

But even that wasn't too bad. Mary was devilishly clever, the way she planted the idea of deeding her own land in Dan's mind. And she did have a type of courage, even though it was prodded and kept alive by money and power, to make her stick it out so long on the very lip of the civilized world. The way they planned it then, they were going to wait until winter and then murder Higgens and arrest me for the crime. But Mary's father hadn't known about the engineering department sending out those two men to make a last-minute check; and before they got away we had them and then went hot-footing up to Mary's to tell her the wonderful news. It was wonderful all right. It changed everything. They didn't have time to ask her father for instructions. They had to work fast, throw away their carefully laid plans and finish us off. Mary and Mixon talked it over, Mixon told Brent to shoot Higgens, and Mary persuaded me to visit town the next day to tell Doc. The rest followed.

I said, "That's a fine story, Mixon. Now we'll head back."

"I am riding to Weeping Water," Mary said coldly.

"You're riding west," I said. "Get on that horse."

She mounted and sat in the saddle, staring at the sky, her mouth anything but firm and lovely. Bring me honey and red watermelon, I thought suddenly, and offer me the sweet words from your lovely mouth.

Dan said, "Jim, you ride the other one. We'll walk."

I didn't argue. I got on Mixon's horse and we headed for home. Mixon walked ahead and Mary followed him. Sam and Dan walked on each side of Mary's horse with a rope tied around her waist and the two ends in their hands. I followed along behind. I could see Sam's face, expressionless and alert. Dan was watching Mixon and moving his lips, and I could see his right hand, holding his rifle, quivering with the pressure of his fingers. He was thinking how they had fooled him, dangled him on a string that had no bottom or top. I wondered what he would do with Mixon when we arrived.

Clancy and five men with extra horses met us about noon, ten miles east of the halfway house; and it was just in time.

Noon, I thought. Twenty-four hours now—or was it an eternity?

We shoved Mixon on a horse and Dan mounted another, and we rode to the halfway house where those same two dirty hostlers were sitting and saying nothing, because three more Bisonette waddies were standing around, keeping an eye on everything. We pushed Mary and Mixon into the small, dirty sod cabin. Clancy closed the door and stared at Mixon, licking his thin, wide lips.

"Town's kinda worked up," Clancy said finally. "Seems like the farmers want to see Mixon bad, Jim."

"That's fine," I said. "I want him to see his old friends again, too."

"Not much law in town," Clancy said. "Folks are riled up."

"Why," I said, "I don't blame them. Just think, Mixon. They missed hanging me by about an hour. I'll bet they've still got the rope knotted and waiting." I laughed. "If you last that long."

Mary said, "No . . ."

"Yes," I said. "They missed one necktie party last night. Now they get ready for a fresh neck."

"You can't do that," Mary said. "Tom didn't shoot Higgens."

"That's thin," I said. "There's no law west of Weeping Water. Mixon hired Brent and you bossed Mixon. We can't hang you because, despite your way of doing things, you're a woman. But, by God, we can do what we like with Mixon. Can't we, Dan?"

"Well," Dan said slowly, "I've been thinking, Jim. I think we ought to let 'em go."

"Both of them?" I asked. "Why, Dan?"

"I can't say it so good," Dan said softly. "But I thought about it while we rode. I know what she is now, and I always knew what he was. That makes them two of a kind.

They're money-hungry and they played us for fools and they lost. They'll blame each other from now on, and they won't ever be able to trust each other with a back turned. They'll go on like that, and some day one of them will throw the other one over. I could kill him with my bare hands and she'd go away and it wouldn't hurt her much. But having him around all the time, knowing he flopped once for her, won't do her a lot of good. And she'll never get rid of him now. She can't. I guess we better let 'em go.''

He had thought it all out in his mind, and in his heart, and I knew he was right. But I wanted one more thing from them. I turned away from them, facing Dan, and winked at him and walked across the room and then swung on them.

"No!" I said. "Mixon is done, Dan."

I wondered if she would rise to the bait. She did. That proved she had some sort of heart, even if it was black as night and incapable of loving anything better than herself—namely, Mixon. She said, "Wait. I'll make you a deal, Jim."

I said, "Yes?"

"Let us go," she said quickly, "and I'll give you my place."

"Well," I said. "That's mighty nice of you, Mary. That makes me think you'll maybe give me your place and we'll have all the land, and then your father will change the route again."

"No," she said. "I promise."

"Your promise!" I said. "It's worth nothing. No, I'll tell you how we'll play this. Deed Dan your place. And now listen to me—if the railroad doesn't come through my front yard next spring, I'll pay you a visit. I'll kill Mixon so fast and so dead you'll see him die before he drops. He could hide on the moon and I'd find him. That's my deal. Now make your promise."

She looked at Mixon, and he was sweating blood. He knew I meant every word, and even if I died before spring, and they crossed us, he'd have Dan and Sam and fifty others to hide from the rest of his life.

She said, "I promise."

"Get out your little treasure box," I said. "I know you've got the title with you. We'll do that right now."

She had that title, all right, hidden on her upper left leg, strapped in place. She filled it out and Clancy and two others witnessed it, just to make sure. Then I made her write a statement that she was not forced into selling for one dollar, and that she would not try to stop us from registering said title when we took it to Weeping Water. Then I had Mixon write out a statement about his activities, how he hired Brent to shoot Higgens, and how Mary's father and Mary were behind everything. While they were writing, I took out the quitclaim deeds and burned them and gave Dan his title. When they finished, I turned to Clancy and said, "Start 'em down the road."

Dan said, "I'll help you start them."

He opened the door and pushed them outside. Clancy gave me a quick glance, and I said, "Watch close and learn something." Clancy grinned at me and hurried after them.

I didn't go outside. I stayed beside the fire and drank hot coffee, five, ten cups full, and watched Sam clean his rifle and shake out his clothing. But I heard plenty of noise outside; and when it died away I opened the door and saw Clancy and two of his men tying Mixon over his saddle and handing the reins to Mary. Clancy said, "Ride!" and they went out of our lives.

It wasn't the way the law would do a job, but where was the law in Spring Valley? We had the land, for the people who would use it decently, and no one was hurt too badly and I liked that. No one was hurt but Higgens and he didn't care now. No one was hurt but little Red and his mother. And that was why I had one more job to do. Just like I had to play that hand with Ellender when I knew he had me beat, I had one more job to finish if I wanted to feel like a man. When you can't use the law to punish a man because that man was the law himself, then you have to make your own laws and act accordingly. Brent was a poor tool in the hands of Mixon and Mary, and perhaps their guilt was greater, but there was another, far greater consideration.

Higgens had been a poor excuse of a man, a bad father to Red. But he was Red's father and Red saw Brent murder him. He had to have something to go on; something he could see and understand. He had to know that a gambler named Stanton, who had played cowboy and Indian with him along the river, and told him a hundred stories, was his friend and his knight in shining armor. He had to have that wonderful feeling of knowing his father was avenged; and only then would he be able to live out his years and feel that his father was not as bad as Brent.

Dan came inside and rubbed his face and grinned. I wanted to hug him, I felt so good about him coming out on top. He'd taken his beating from Mary and tasted it, and had his own private hell, and then he threw it all away like the tawdry gilt it was, and came out stronger and cleaner and bigger than ever. It took a man to do that job—and Dan was all man.

I said, "Clancy, let's ride!"

Late afternoon; almost six o'clock and almost thirty hours for me. Time running smooth and unfelt through our hearts.

They were waiting for us at the store, about twenty people. We rode off the trail and dismounted and I saw Charlotte and her father standing on the front steps. I went over and looked at him and extended my hand. He never hesitated; he took it and we shook.

"Good party?" he asked.

"Fine," I said. "Everything worked out the way we wanted. Thanks for all your help."

"Hah," he said. "That was a pleasure. Where are they?"

I told him all about catching them and the way Dan figured things out. He mulled it over and shook his head. "Best way," he said. "Killing never solved anything, Jim."

Charlotte took my hands and smiled, and said. "Are you all right, Jim?"

"Never better," I grinned. "Little tired but still kicking."

"And Sam?" she said. "And Dan?"

"You can't kill Sam," I said. "Why don't you go ask Dan yourself?"

She got red and turned away to where Dan was talking with Clancy and the other men. I looked at Bisonette and saw the twinkle in his eyes. I said, "Where's Doc?"

"In town with some sick-feeling farmers," he said. "And my boys."

"And Brent?" I asked softly.

"In town," he said. "In the jail, with his guns on." He hesitated. "That's how you told us you wanted it."

"That's how," I said. "I've got a deal for you, Bisonette. Let's warm up a little while I tell you, and then we'll ride to town."

He said, "Fire in the stove. Your hands look cold."

We sat in the kitchen and I peeled off my wet clothing and toweled myself dry and red, and dressed in clean underwear and a soft shirt and my corduroy pants and good boots. I cleaned my guns and got a full box of cartridges

from my valise and reloaded with new shells. Then I read-
justed my holsters and got them settled under my coat, and
stood over the fire, warming my hands, and told Bisonette
what I had in mind.

I wanted to sell him my property for ten thousand cash
and a fifty-fifty split on all profits above that, received from
lot sales when the railroad came through. I wanted him to
advise Dan on all business when the boom started, and
explained about Dan having Mary's place now. He grinned
knowingly and I told him to send plenty of men with Dan
when he registered the deed in Weeping Water. And then
I told him the whole story, just to make sure he understood
everything. And when I finished, I said, "Now, I want to
apologize for being a fool."

"No," he said. "I'm a fool, too, Jim. I was stubborn
myself. I misjudged you in the beginning. Now I know.
I'll accept your deal on the land, but I don't see why you
can't stay and help us build this valley."

I tapped my chest. "I'd like to, but not yet. Now, let's
sign the papers and you can give me a check or some
cash"—I grinned—"I can use a little hard cash."

So we made out the papers once more, only this time it
was a good, clean feeling. Bisonette had a thousand cash
in the general store safe and five thousand on the ranch.
He would get the thousand for me in town and give me a
check on his bank in Weeping Water. I called Dan inside
and he and Charlotte came together, smiling at each other.
I told them what we had done.

Charlotte said, "You're going, Jim?"

"Not this minute," I said. "We'll ride to town first.
I've got a job to do, and I want to see Doc and make some
arrangements."

Dan said, "Charlotte, you better stay here."

He didn't know that girl. She said, "I'll ride along."

There was nothing more to say. My hands were warm

and my mind was cold. I slipped on my mittens and said, "Let's ride."

Have you killed a man? Do you know how it feels? In war or in fair fight? If you have, you know how I felt. If you haven't, you'll never understand. I've read a lot of books in which the killing of men has been described. You can never get it down on paper. I'd killed before. I had to. And it felt the same way every time. The first one was the man who shot my father. Then the war, and I don't remember the times. And after that, through the years and on the long, endless trails, I'd had to keep it up to live. And now I was tired, and weary of it all. But not too tired for one last time.

We rode into the south end of town and I stopped and thought, Make it in the open, on the street. Make this one the last one, and make it quick.

You can't allow yourself to think it might be you. I never did.

I turned to them and said, "Better move over on the sidewalk—Clancy . . ."

He rode up beside me, unsmiling. I said, "Ride ahead and send him into the street."

Clancy nodded and spurred his black up Main. I dismounted and took off my mittens and handed them and the reins to Dan.

I said, "It's warming up, Dan."

"Some," Dan said quietly. "We'll have a good day tomorrow."

Sam looked at me and wiggled his rifle and I knew what he meant; take one for him. Then I turned and started up the street.

I saw Doc in front of the drugstore, and beside him, holding Doc's left arm, was Red. He looked at me and I knew what he was thinking—that here was the end of the playing under the trees and fishing in the river and swiping melons in the fields. He had to see this, and he would never be the same again, but he would be a better man. He would be a better man because Brent was the kind of man who hated children, and had been caught and would be destroyed by a child.

I was a block from the jail when the door opened and Brent stepped outside. He pushed at his guns and pulled his hat low over his eyes and looked around. He saw the people thick behind store windows, and between stores. He saw Doc and he saw Red, and he jerked that way and Clancy's voice floated gently down the street:

"Straight ahead, Brent!"

He saw me coming up the street. He moved away from the jail into the middle of the street, and I wondered if he was thinking about the beginning of everything and how he had started up the long trail and could never go back.

He lifted his hands to his chest and rubbed them together and dropped them, arms stiff, to his sides. He walked toward me. I knew he'd be thinking that he couldn't get away, but if he kept walking and didn't draw, he might get me so close he couldn't miss even if I killed him while he shot.

I let him come to forty feet. Then I stopped and said, "Now, Brent!" and watched him stop and curse me wordlessly for outthinking him.

He went for his guns.

I never made a better draw in my life, with sleepless, terrible hours behind me. I drew the right gun first and shot three times before I drew the left gun and used it. He got his right .44 belt high when my first bullet struck him, and he fired one shot into the snowy street as he fell. He never got the left .44 out of its holster. I shot him six times before he hit the ground.

Then I went over to the drugstore where Doc and Red stood together, and I put my hand on Red's shoulder and

Doc smiled at us. People moved into the street, and their voices rose around and over us.

I said, "Doc, I've got to ride."

Doc said, "Where?"

"To Weeping Water," I said. "And beyond. Down the river to New Orleans, then to Santa Fe. I know a house there, Doc. Maybe I'm crazy, but I keep thinking you want to ride along. Drugstores are good anywhere. A doctor is needed anywhere. It's high and dry, and cool and quiet. You can sleep late and sit in the sun, and when I feel like I'm a man again, we can go on from there."

"It's a funny coincidence," Doc said softly, "but I was speculating along those same lines. When do we leave?"

"We'll finish everything today," I said. "We can make Weeping Water tomorrow night and take the train south that same night. We'll travel light."

It was cold the next morning but the sky was a shining blue. We said good-bye at the store. Charlotte kissed both of us. Dan wanted to come but something new was holding him. We shook hands all around. Bisonette was sending ten men with us, to make sure we weren't harmed. Sam Ronson said, "Mebbe I'll take me one more ride next spring, if you got room?"

I said, "We'll have room," and we mounted and rode down the path to the river and splashed across the ford. I turned in the saddle when we topped the east ridge. The last thing I saw was the store roof, white under the sun beside the river.